Christmas at the Cross

Maeve Murphy

Bridge House

British Library Cataloguing in Publication Data
A Record of this Publication is available from the British
Library

ISBN 978-1-914199-06-6

This edition published 2021 by Bridge House Publishing
Manchester, England

Cover photograph © Tobias Newland

Christmas at the Cross

Dedicated to my husband Richard

Contents

Foreword by Aidan Andrew Dun

Kings Cross, at the heart of London, is a zone of power. William Blake made the Cross the centre of his London cosmology. W. B. Yeats lived here for twenty-three years, the years in which the hermetic lunar system underpinning A Vision was transmitted (through his wife) to the poet. And Arthur Rimbaud, the messianic teenage seer who today may justifiably be called planetary poet-laureate, wrote in Kings Cross many of his Illuminations and much of his confessional Season in Hell.

There are many external factors in the theory of Kings Cross as shamanic threshold, interface between the worlds, omphalos. The zone is circled by megalithic fire-hills: Primrose Hill, Parliament Hill, St Michael's Mount and the Penton of Pentonville – underneath which lies Merlin's Cave. And fire above is mirrored by water below: a sacred river once ran through the Cross. She was known as the Old River of Wells, named for her many healing sources which survived as spas until the Georgian period. As the Fleet – commemorated in Fleet Street – she was buried alive in the mid-to-late eighteenth century.

In Maeve Murphy's *Christmas at the Cross*, set in the squatyards and badlands of North West One, a 'free-falling woman' – barely more than a teenager – narrates a mordant tale shot through with defilement and degradation, yet mysteriously edged with something like salvation. On the run from a demon-flame, hiding out among sex-workers and drug-fiends, she perceives the latter as almost angelic compared to her psychotic ex-lover. We are reminded of Arthur Rimbaud's disturbing candour when he says, at the climax of Season in Hell 'I saw the damnation of lying couples down there.' Here is a dark river in flood, a swollen

9

torrent of confessional debris washing up against unexpected islands of innocence. At one point in the plunge towards some urban event horizon, as carol singers shake buckets for the Christmas homeless and a suicidal urge surfaces in the narrator, a small donkey enters the narrative as if to emphasize that we are being sucked into a metropolitan black hole where incongruities live side-by-side. Above Ave Marias and ambulance sirens, breaking glass and Velvet Underground tracks we seem to hear Rimbaud's desperate cry 'The Gospel! The Gospel has gone by!'

In the backstreets of Kings Cross stands a mysterious tumulus. On this small hill stands St Pancras Old Church, named the 'head and mother of all Christian churches' in secret Vatican archive documents, the possible seed-foundation of the Celtic Church. Ask most Londoners about this church and one draws a blank; it's dedication is even more obscure. Yet Pancras – as patron saint of teenagers and patron saint of truth – is a cosmological figure whose iconography is significant. Pancras corresponds to the child-demiurge of many creation-myths. For instance in the ancient Chinese model of origins an androgynous Pan Ku creates the oceans from 'his' blood and the mountains from 'his' bones, the vegetation from 'his' hair and human beings from the lice of 'his' armpit. Until, destroyed, exhausted by the act of creation, the teenage god/goddess collapses, self-martyred.

Murphy's young singer/songwriter Blathnaid – pronounced Bla-nid – an independent young woman on a life-threatening journey to truth, carries the archetypes of the sunchild Pancras.

As Murphy's novella makes dark headway, against a backdrop of Christmas lights drinking-sessions end in assault and disaster. Now heroin is the only way to invoke that totality which died with the sunchild. Now Class A drugs are the only substitute for God. Little Flower (as 'Blathnaid' translates) is making a crossing of the night-sea where those who don't grasp that suffering is universal drown in self-pity, go under in sacrificial waves. We see her near-martyrdom, hospitalized at the equinox. We also see her tempted to go the hard road of the hooker who has her revenge by 'making all men pay'. Yet we also track her participation in a church-led street-girl resistance-movement in which the 'bad' girls challenge the brutality of the police who rule North West One with terror and impunity. We sense her growing compassion for the 'scagheads and prossies' whose fate is even more desperate than her own. In spite of her individual harrowing we realize that Blathnaid is discovering a special kind of freedom by choosing a response to life not based in blind reactivity. And her determination to change herself is a strong antidote to the deadliness and negativity of her experience. In a Gandhian sense it is world-transforming.

Even without a hard-hitting text to power the storyline I would have been fascinated by the outsider themes and site-specific detail of *Christmas at the Cross*. Yet I immediately recognized the authentic edge of a narrative driven by street idiom and the openness of an acute observer. Sequences in the work remind me of events which had either happened to me or to people I knew in the derries. (Like Maeve Murphy's Little Flower I fell under the spell of the Cross once-upon-a-time, descending into a personal inferno in this zone of London.) In *Christmas at the Cross* I quickly discerned that familiar raw wonderment which is often all that is left when a lifechanging windstorm has blown through a comfortable existence. Yet I also detected larger resonances; the story seemed to carry greater embodiments and symbolisms. The presence in the tale of a Japanese sage and an 'Indian princess' already moved the narrative into cross-cultural territory. But it was the name 'Blathnaid' – once I had learned to pronounce it correctly – that suddenly triggered other dimensionalities and meanings. Clearly this ancient Irish name easily shifts into 'planet'. Now the Gothic trope of young woman on the run from a psychopath morphs into the matricidal tragedy of our times: the psychotic assault on the mother of us all – holy earth – the rape of nature by mechanized technology.

Maeve Murphy's tale of a young woman's wild quest for equilibrium can be read as an urban parable of modern times, and her parable can be extended to imply the salvation of the earth. Struggles of gritty souls like Blathnaid will undoubtedly move humankind towards Blake's Jerusalem, and the truthful telling of her dark history should open many eyes.

In *Christmas at the Cross* Murphy is suggesting that non-reactivity is the only spiritual response to the world's hellish face. At one juncture in the narrative, when anger at perceived wrongs is rising in Blathnaid, when she's at the point of boiling over into rage, her wise Japanese friend says to her: The bad people help you change your karma. That's it. It's a non-dualistic way of looking at things.

It's the only way of looking at things.

Aidan Andrew Dun is the author of the epic poem Vale Royal *whose subject matter is both the psychogeography of Kings Cross and the mysteries of the transcultural sunchild.*

Introduction

I had always wanted to write a book. I had written a short story, published by Bridge water and then The Irish Times in Christmas 2019 and then when lock down happened in 2020 and film making was in chaos, I knew I had been thrown a rare opportunity. And took it.

The novel and story are a work of fiction, inspired from when I lived in Kings Cross, as a young woman at a crucial crossroads in my early to mid twenties. Inspiration came from the people I met, or things I heard or saw or was told. Outsider people often young women, who often didn't have a voice, or were under the radar. Kings Cross at that time, is etched in my brain. I was aware for many they were passing through, like the trains arriving and departing. Many people got stuck. Some tragically died or vanished, which haunted. It may sound like a contradiction as the area was notorious as a red light district, and dangerous as a centre of drug crime, but honestly I met some of the best and most decent people ever during that time. The feeling of friendship between young women and community, maybe because of the real challenges, was amazing. The fighting spirit and comraderie and at times a decisive sense of "enough" existed in part because of those connections.

Of course Kings Cross today is a transformed place. And we were so young. I hope all who have an edgy period in their youth, especially young women, get the opportunity to transform it and get older.

Maeve Murphy

Part I

Christmas at the Cross

Kings Cross, early nineties

I posted the letter into the red letterbox.

There was a dusked bloodshot shell-shocked sky hanging over the St Pancras skyline. The street was empty; an ominous silence. Then came the sound of dogs barking, viciously spilling out onto the street. A Japanese man walked out of the courtyard opposite. I walked back, up the stairwell and into my flat.

Okay it was the pits. There's no point denying it. I mean I could say it was some kind of lifestyle choice, some kind of protest. But I was lost, totally lost, that was the truth of it. Dazed, concussed, staggering like a three-legged dog trying to find its way, blinded by a dazzling razor of winter sunlight, deafened by the bleating of car horns.

I was twenty-three, alone, adrift, and living in the shite hole of Kings Cross. A spit, a wink and a toss away from the scagheads and prossies. A free-falling woman. Oh yes, sexual desire had brought my downfall. Fate had knocked me; not quite unconscious but I was spaced out, floating in cotton wool. My life set on a timer, ticking away, finally had blown up. Trapped in the debris, I couldn't get out. If I went 'home' I would end up doing what my parents wanted. *I* wanted to play music and be a musician. I was a musician. But since meeting Kieran I had stopped even doing that.

I was consumed by Kieran.

I'd been deluding myself that my increasing decreasing situation was interesting, life on the margins. And now as I sat in my shitty sleazy flat, on the torn, ripped sofa with bits of yellow foam bleeding out, I was in shock. Something terrible had happened and I had posted a letter. I had referenced the attack to the attacker. But what would happen now?

My neck still hurt. It was the run-up to Christmas and I hadn't posted my cards yet.

Last night I had gone to bed and left Kieran next door in the sitting room of his new flat in Liverpool. I felt a bit heady because of the joint we'd smoked. He'd had coke too. I fell asleep quickly. Then a couple of hours later I was woken by Kieran pouncing on me, waking me, throttling me. I remember the shock. A feeling of raw fear spreading rapidly. Inner panic.

"No," I said, trying to stay calm. He was in a dream and would wake up.

"Yes," he said.

It was that 'yes' that was terrifying. It was cool, deliberate and conscious. His quiet Liverpool accent sounded threatening for the first time. I tried to push him off but he was a big man. It was impossible. Unstoppable.

"Stop it, please, you're hurting me!" I couldn't breathe. The air was getting darker. My head was getting lighter. He let go.

I walked into the toilet, shaking. Was it because in the pub I persuaded him not to get involved in a fight? Kieran had a glass in his hand, ready to smash it. I told him the police would be called. Had I made him, the tough guy, run away from a fight? Was he in rage over that? Adrenalised from that? My fault then. I'd stopped him. Was that it?

In the loo I heard the sound of the front door being locked. My head whirled. I could stay in there but I thought I would attempt normality, so I went back in to the bedroom and he instructed me to give him a blow job. Terrified, I complied.

I must have then slept. He must have been there. All I

remember is this morning waking up and feeling very calm, almost at peace, kind of floating. He was lying beside me, but I had my back to him. I remember feeling this very tender kiss on my back. I didn't respond, just lay there, not wanting to speak. Kieran got up and made me breakfast, something he had never done before. A fry-up of sausages and bacon and eggs.

In my cotton wool world, I had breakfast with him. Then he walked me to the train station. The last thing he said to me yesterday was, "It'll harden you."

It was absolutely chilling. A full admission. No remorse. Yes, he was saying, he'd ground my face in the mud, stamped on it and somehow that was a good thing. He was the boss.

Only three months before I had been living in a beauty of a flat in Camden Town. Spacious, with wooden beam floors and white walls. Camden has a wonderful way of tying everything together with a bonhomie boho bow. I was having a good time, being young, not thinking about much else. I was so caught up with Kieran and his *show bizz* friends. It was exciting, like being around them made me really successful as well. Sex and coke and late-night Soho.

I didn't notice that my flatmate had missed her last three rent cheques. I couldn't afford to pay her rent as well or the deposit for another flat. Rory, a guy I vaguely knew from a late-night Greek restaurant in Chalk Farm, was going travelling for a year. As long as the Housing Association didn't find out, I could stay in his flat, up four flights of stairs in a condemned red-brick Victorian East End dwelling called Midhope House.

Having now posted the letter, and back inside, I sat in fog-filled shock, chain-smoking on the ripped sofa and staring into space. I shouldn't have sent it. I felt like the walls were slanting, narrowing, tilting across, closing in on me.

The phone rang. I jumped. A college friend, Ava. I tried to tell her what had happened. She said something about weird things can happen in relationships. Really? I finished the call. Ava had a new job, was getting married, she was busy. Too busy.

I still hadn't cried.

I got up. Night had fallen. I don't know how many hours had passed. The Italians were whistling their drug-selling code to each other outside. I never quite worked it out: if it was to warn each other if cops were about, or whether it was to let them know of some more *stuff*. They had their mad wee rituals anyway – people nodding to other people and then some runner stuffing the gear somewhere for the pick-up. The black guys did the crack; they kind of opted for the deft hand-to-mouth, or hand-to-anus technique. To be honest, when I first moved in, I always thought those guys, with their hooded tops, standing in packs near York Way, looked like they were acting the hard men in some New York film. But that rose-tinted thought quickly evaporated when I saw some beat the shit out of a guy in an alley. They weren't acting. They were just really fucking mean.

I got up and looked out the window.

Opposite, down below, just outside the entrance of the other Housing-Association-come-squat, near a streetlamp, was a tall, thin Asian woman, leaning against the wall, smoking a cigarette. I stared. There we were… I sat back down on the sofa.

There was a knock on the door. My heart rate turned up a notch. Through the weird fisheye lens, I saw it was the prostitute that had been on the street, under the street lamp. A little frightened, I opened the door a tiny bit.

"What is it?" She had such an intense presence, penetrating, staring eyes. Nothing about her was trying to please, but there was a kind of tenderness about her. She had black bags under her eyes, stood thin in her Lycra black mini dress. She was beautiful, her features were delicate but her skin was rough. London Asian, that was unusual for a prostitute.

"Can you spare a couple of quid?"

So here I was, Lady Muck, literally. But it made me feel good to feel kind of superior in my compassion. I felt for her. I wasn't her. I went into the sitting room and took out a couple of quid that I didn't have to give away and handed them to her. She looked at me. Her brown eyes had a depth. The weird thing about Kings Cross is that the people who lived there, never made eye contact with the prostitutes and they never made eye contact with us.

"All I have," I replied.

I was different from her. I was not in her dreadful situation.

"Cheers." She replied in a lazy London way. Was I different from her?

I watched her shuffling out of the stairwell and down the road, passing a guy walking his bike in. Yesterday I was. Today I wasn't so sure.

The guy looked up and saw me with my face up against the window. I quickly moved away.

The next day I woke up hungry, tired, still scared. My dole cheque had not arrived, no money, other than shrapnel. Enough maybe for some fags and some Marathons which were cheap and filling. All I could think about was food. I rubbed my legs with my hands, because they felt so cold. A woman was going hysterical, screaming outside and someone screamed at her to shut up. I lifted the bit of cloth over the window and peeked out. It was that girl who had knocked on my door.

Poverty, I tell you, is the most soul-destroying thing. You spend your whole time thinking about what you can't have, and seeing as basically money and beauty are the only two things most people seem to value, then you are the lowest of the low if you don't have either, an invisible. I would say both a skewed romantic-type socialism and maybe some eastern mystics got it terribly wrong. There is nothing praiseworthy in poverty. It tightens your life to a point of rigidity and decisions are made from that cramped tense state of mind and often not wise ones. The police had by now arrived and finished talking to that girl and let her go. Her pimp or whoever the tracksuit guy was, stayed on talking to the police. I lowered the cloth on the window and got dressed.

I managed to speak to my sister on the phone.

"…why don't you talk to a priest?"

"A priest?"

That was kind of a weird thought. I wasn't sure about that.

I went out. I walked to the grey stone church at the bottom of Cromer Street. I was always trying to be a good person. I felt permanently at fault and always the one to blame. In Lady Muck mode I felt I should do my bit to help the poor down and outs of Kings Cross. I also had like a pain in my stomach which I ignored.

I walked down the stone steps and through the iron gates of the basement of the church which led to the kitchen. I entered the main room. I looked at the mostly old men, battered by life. Fallen through the cracks. A lot of them were Irish, sitting around the tables, having charity soup and a sandwich. I felt their silent shame. I looked at the red tinsel Christmas decorations hanging on the wall.

19

There was a small wooden nativity scene on the side. The figures of Mary and Joseph in the stable with the little baby Jesus in the crib with bits of artificial straw. Beside them were the Magi, the figures of the three wise kings bearing gifts. And some wooden sheep. I wasn't going home for Christmas, neither was anyone here.

I went up to the counter which was a few enamel tables put together.

"Do you need any volunteers, to help serve food? Over Christmas?"

The guy at the counter glanced at me. He held out the plate of sandwiches.

"Would you like some soup with it?"

"I was offering to help," I said, mortified. I also recognised him as the guy walking his bike from last night.

He kind of smiled and looked vaguely apologetic but continued to offer me the sandwich and soup. With burning cheeks, I turned on my heel and left the building.

As I crossed the road, a tramp on his way in to get some food spontaneously hugged me. There I was in the middle of Kings Cross, being hugged by a tramp and it made me strangely happy. Maybe I was like St Francis of Assisi.

I carried on walking and went 'home'. I sat on the pathetic ripped, brown, corduroy sofa with bits of yellow sponge coming out. I had planned to cover the sofa with a tablecloth. But I sat instead, staring at the window, not enough energy. I could sort this out myself. I just needed some session work. Or write some songs to sell.

I chain-smoked about ten cigarettes in an hour. I counted all my small change, ten pence, five pence and copper, enough for another box of ten.

I walked down the several flights of stairs, bought my fags in the Asian supermarket on Cromer and was heading back when I walked straight into the guy who had offered me the soup and a sandwich. I tried to pretend I didn't see him.

"I offer everyone who comes in a free sandwich!"

I turned and laughed. No point being uppity. I noticed the warmth of his brown eyes. They were lovely. There was a sparkle of wit in them. I liked his husky London accent.

"Do you work at the church every day?"

"Only occasionally."

"Do you live round here?"

"Yeah, I'm flat-minding for someone... I'm on Midhope."

"I live there too."

"Really?"

My jaw nearly dropped.

"Yes. On the ground floor."

I was amazed someone like him lived so near.

"I'm on the fifth floor," I said.

"I'm just going back there."

"Me too. What's your name?" We walked together.

"David. Yours?"

"Blathnaid," I replied. "Bla, like blah blah and nid, like lid."

"Lovely... what does it mean?"

"Little flower."

We both laughed. I don't know why it was funny. It just kind of was. Maybe it was a funny place to be a little flower.

"Did you know two people were found dead of an overdose a couple of days ago in Tankerton?"

That was the next building over. I shook my head. "No, I didn't know that, not my thing: heroin."

We carried on walking. I had this strange urge to hold his hand. He asked me what I was up to. I told him I was a musician but I was thinking of writing a play. A musical. About Hiroshima. He glanced at me, to see if I was serious, and judging that I was, suggested I talk to Yoichi who lived

21

in the second courtyard across. His mother had survived the Hiroshima attack as a young woman.

"Really?"

He laughed. I asked him what he did, when he wasn't doing the homeless food thing. He told me that he took photographs and that occasionally they showed in national newspapers, but he was finding it hard to earn a living. I nodded. Like me.

David felt like a log in the middle of a crazy sea. And he was reminding me that there was dry land, a shore...

David and I reached the place where we lived. He headed towards his flat.

"I'll drop Yoichi's phone number through your door."

I nodded. Even in my dazed state I clocked that gorgeous smile that broke David's serious face wide open. It was nice to know he was close. I plodded back up the stairs. I became aware again of this pain in my stomach. I ignored it.

I got in and lay in the bath. Unable to move. Motionless.

A knock on the door. It was dark now.

"Blathnaid, are you in there?" Kieran's voice.

I didn't move. I didn't breathe. The knock continued.

I was now shaking. I held my breath.

"I got your letter this morning. Came down on the train... open up, love."

For a split second I wanted to open the door. The way he said "love" was tender. Loving even. Familiar. Maybe this could all be okay. I didn't open the door. I lay in the bath shaking. Finally, I heard his steps as he moved away and walked down the stairwell. I heard him stop and then continue.

I got up out of the bath and wrapped a towel around me. I went to the window. I could see him walking away down the street. Relief.

The phone rang. I picked it up.

"Hello?"

The line went dead. I knew it was Kieran.

I would go to the police tomorrow. I didn't care if that was not the thing the Northern Irish Catholics do. I just didn't care. Now I would go to bed, not think about it.

I then took a heavy wooden chair and placed it on top of another chair against the door. That didn't feel enough, so I took the really nice wicker basket which had all my shoes and placed it on top of the chairs against the door.

The phone rang again. The phone kept ringing. I didn't touch it.

Then it stopped. There was silence. Beautiful silence.

I could finally sink into the silence and sleep.

The following morning my dole cheque arrived. I felt such joy. I had control back in my life. I walked down the post office just opposite Kings Cross Station and cashed it, posted my Christmas cards and bought some chocolate Hobnobs as a kind of treat. On my way back I passed the big group of prostitutes standing shivering outside the post office.

A police car slowly pulled up. A policeman suddenly opened the car door and dragged a very young woman who was just standing there and pushed her and shoved her really roughly into the police car.

That horrible energy clung to me as I headed home. Crossing the road, I walked back down the narrow back streets to Hillview, into a courtyard near mine and up the stairs and along a balcony. I knocked on a freshly-painted door. A Japanese guy opened it. David had slipped Yoichi's number underneath my door. He looked younger than I thought he would be, early forties, shiny, kind of joyful, very clear eyes. I walked in and saw a modest flat, in good

23

nick, sparsely but nicely decorated. Carpet on the floor, a TV and a big brown wooden box or casket with brass knob handles on a small table. I was intrigued by the wooden box, my eyes drawn to it. It felt religious. I wondered if I was taking my sister's advice after all and going to see a priest.

Yoichi asked me if I would like a cup of tea or coffee. I asked if he had a green tea, he said he only had PG tips. I explained I was interested in doing a play about Hiroshima. He asked why? I said I was very interested in survivors' stories. It might be musical as I was a musician, so kind of like Noh theatre. I said it would probably need Japanese actors and musicians; it wouldn't be like Mickey Rooney in *Breakfast at Tiffany's*. Yoichi laughed, he thought this was hilarious.

He told me about his mum's experience, about how the Hiroshima bomb had happened in an instant. Everyone was just going about their ordinary lives with no expectation of it; how there was a flash of light. His mum said there were dead people lying everywhere. And everything was covered in black ash. People were lying side by side inside public buildings. He said there were maggots coming out of the living who were not yet dead and they were in great pain. As soon as the maggots appeared people knew they were probably going to die. His mother did suffer radiation sickness, was in hospital, very weak and she kept fainting. He said many people committed suicide and his mum said she was tempted but she thought about her family.

"Yes," I said, jotting down a few notes into a notepad. I could hear a tune in my head.

"Does your mum feel bitter about her experience, her karma? Her like punishment."

Yoichi laughed. "You believe people terrible 'sinner' who deserves punishment?"

24

I didn't know how to reply.

"I believe in the law of cause and effect. That's karma. So, for example, if you don't respect your life and you keep making those causes to not respect your life, then your life will not be respected."

This was intellectually interesting, way better than a priest. Yoichi was looking at me. I hid my neck with my hand. I knew there were bruises. I had seen them.

"So, it is people's fault what happens to them?"

He picked up one of my chocolate hobnobs and took a bite. "People who hurt someone else are accountable for their actions."

I nodded.

"How does your mum feel about the pilot who dropped that bomb?"

"She's not attached to him. My mum knows her karma is her karma and the bomber's karma is his karma. She has to deal with her karma and he has to deal with his karma. If he wishes. Separate."

I found this fascinating.

"My mother now make her karma her mission."

I felt woozy.

"Mission?" That word made me think of the missions in Africa, of black babies.

"So she doesn't want to just kill him?"

"No. She work for peace."

I switched off. "Your mum's a saint... not everyone can be as good as that."

Yoichi chuckled. I got up and glanced at the wooden box. He watched me.

"I'm a Catholic," I said.

"Better speak to a priest then." His clear almond eyes were dancing, teasing me.

"Maybe I will."

"Drop the self-pity," he said staring at me.

I wanted at that moment to smash his happy, shiny face. What a bastard! At least a Catholic priest would hear your sins and give you absolution. I didn't want to hear his heartless eastern clap-trap anymore. I sprung to my feet.

"Well, Yoichi, I better go. Better conversation than you normally get in confession, that's all I can say."

"Three Our Father and Two Hail Mary!" he replied.

As I walked down the stairwell, I became aware again of the pain. I touched my hand on my lower abdomen. It felt bloated, hard. I'd take some more painkillers when I got in. That's what I was thinking about as I turned the corner. *Did I have enough? Should I go the shops? No – there were enough—*

And there he was.

At the top of the stairs to my floor.

He was standing outside my door.

And he had seen me.

I wasn't sure whether to turn and run or to keep walking. Kieran looked at me, he didn't look angry. He looked normal. He smiled, like he was pleased to see me. What was really attractive when we first met was he really saw me, asked me questions about me, though never actually came to see me play, up until recently I had been doing small pub gigs. I noticed he looked his age, forty, normally I never thought about that much.

"I called round yesterday."

I nodded. Didn't make any comment.

He waited for me to open the door. I didn't.

"I've just remembered I've got an appointment at the doctor," I said.

"Are you okay?" His eyes were piercing, though his manner was friendly.

"Yes, I think so."

"Look where you're living. Jesus, Blathnaid. I got your letter… So what actually happened?"

I looked at him, gobsmacked not knowing what to say. He didn't remember? Really?

"I just know something terrible happened."

He looked sincere. "What happened?"

"You…"

Finding it hard to say more words, I pointed to my bruised neck. He looked away, looked disturbed.

"I'm sorry." He sounded sincere.

But was he? He said it would "harden" me.

Maybe I did need to speak to a priest. Focus on forgiving?

"It's Christmas. I'm meeting a few people for drinks up in the pub tonight, if you want to come up later?"

He was brushing this all off like it was nothing. He said he would see me later. I nodded. He kissed me. It was just like a normal kiss.

"I love you," he whispered. He had never actually said that before.

Maybe love could conquer all. He had just lost it, though I still didn't know why, but everyone deserves a second chance. Don't they?

I walked through the pub door a few hours later. Kieran was sitting at a table with a couple of other guys. There was a Channel 4 documentary person too, hanging out in the London Irish scene which was Kieran's thing. It was exciting to be so near these people. It made me feel like I wasn't just on the dole, I was part of it. Maybe I could

27

do some incidental music for it. If I could pluck up the nerve to discuss that with them. I also had to be careful, Kieran sometimes got jealous. Kieran looked nice in his denim shirt. I wore a black polo neck top. There was a large real Christmas tree along the back wall and a show band on the stage. It was packed. People were up in festive spirit, dancing away to country and western cover songs.

"Have you brought me a blow-up doll for me Christmas present?" Kieran asked.

It was such a gross thing to say on so many levels, it should have sent me out the door.

Kieran then talked about me going to spend time with him again in Liverpool. I couldn't understand all these conflicting things, so I went to the ladies and reapplied my lipstick. I needed time to think.

On my way back came I heard Kieran talking to one of the guys. They had their backs to me.

"I hope you didn't mind Blathnaid joining us. I want to have a sweet night tonight. Know what I mean? Butter her up."

A throaty male chuckle erupted between them all.

My cheeks burned. Something snapped. All the stuff I'd kept hidden away from myself was now erupting. Running, backwards, forwards, round my brain.

There is a truth.

Don't say too much.

I will! I'LL SCREAM!

I picked up my red wine; threw it over him. I had such rage the glass shattered in my hands and now there was glass all over the floor, and everyone looking at me. That's when I saw the blood; dripping from my hand, red blood and soon it had become a red hand. I felt sweat on my face, a heavy pain pulsing. He jumped out of his seat and came forward to console me, to calm me down.

"GET AWAY FROM ME!" I roared.

He took a step closer.

"DON'T YOU COME NEAR ME OR I'LL PHONE THE POLICE!"

Next thing I was pushing open the door. And then I was running.

It was raining. I was bawling. Like a junkie I'd gone back to what had hurt me – like an old habit. I hated myself. I couldn't be stronger. I couldn't make better choices. I couldn't change, so my life would never change. I was stuck like this. Stuffed. I screamed. It ripped the air.

The rest is a daze. I remember sitting in the tube carriage, blood streaming out of my hand. A guy further down had blood all over his white shirt. He was sitting upright, looking straight ahead as if he was fine.

I got out of the tube at Kings Cross. There were a group of people singing carols and collecting money in buckets for the homeless. Traffic on Euston Road was buzzing past. I stepped out into the road.

That's when a hand reached out and grabbed me back as a huge lorry drove past. I looked round to see Yoichi's face. He looked furious. I was stunned. How the hell was he there? Was he like monkey from that Japanese TV series? He snatched me across the road, into the Burger King opposite just beside the post office which was alive with all the usual illicit late-night stuff. Just as we entered, I saw the Asian prostitute I'd lent a couple of quid to. She was there, shivering with the rest of them.

Next thing I knew, the young African girl behind the counter was cleaning my hand with ice and then wrapping it in kitchen roll.

The face of the Asian prostitute loomed before me, looking concerned.

"Is she okay?" she asked Yoichi, "I know her."

"What's your name?" I asked.

"Nadina. What's yours?"

"Blathnaid. It means 'little flower'."

We all laughed until a pimp appeared with horrible dead darting eyes, wanting to know what was going on.

Yoichi then briskly walked me out and back in the direction of my flat.

When we reached Midhope Street, we passed David returning from a night out. He looked at me.

"You okay?"

"Fuck off!"

I didn't want him to see me like this. I could see the shock in his eyes. His eyes. His beautiful warm lovely eyes. I felt like crying, all I wanted to do was talk to him. See him. Speak with him. Find out about him. Everything about him. David quickly opened his flat and went in.

Yoichi and I got up the stairs to my flat. The pain in my abdomen was now unbearable. It was coming in waves. I was bent over holding it with my bleeding hand.

I got out my key and opened the flat door. Yoichi was still with me.

"Want a cup of tea?"

Yoichi was looking at me strangely. I went into the narrow kitchen to make it.

"Blathnaid," he said quietly but in an alarmed way. He looked at my legs.

I looked down. Blood. Clumps, black, clotted. A pounding in my ears. That is when I collapsed. All I remember was an ambulance man arriving and I was half carried out and down the stairs by him and Yoichi. I passed

Mike, a junkie who lived below and was standing at his door with his pink-shaded glasses and holding his scrawny black cat.

"Has she OD-ed?"

The guy from New Zealand who was an artist, who lived opposite Mike, opened and then quickly shut his door when he saw what was going on.

We got to the bottom of the stairs. All I could think about was David but his door did not open. I'd just told him to fuck off. I really was a stupid bitch.

I was put on a stretcher. I heard the hushed word 'miscarriage'. I had missed a period. The ambulance driver asked me if Yoichi was my next of kin.

"I'm a neighbour," he said.

"Is there a next of kin, we need a number and address?"

"No next of kin, no room at the inn…" I mumbled.

David's face and eyes loomed in front of mine. He *was* there. His eyes were so warm but he looked scared. So was I. A baby? I was really losing a baby?

"Come over when you get back."

He took my hand.

They lifted me into the ambulance.

I could see the tiny little narrow alley to the side.

A half-eaten hamburger and a used condom lay on the ground.

I suddenly saw it all so clearly. This was hell. I had to get out.

The ambulance drove off.

Blue light swirling into the darkness.

Another Kings Cross casualty. But I swore to my life as we raced through the streets, I would change.

Ave Maria was playing somewhere.

It was now Christmas Eve.

Maiden hear a maiden's sorrow,
Mother hear a suppliant child...

I could still feel the warmth of David's heart in my hand.

I held on tightly to that.

Part II

The Little Statue

My Aunty Pat was avoided.

Everything around her was steeped in disapproval. When she rang up and spoke in her weird English Irish accent, we all didn't want to talk to her. When I was a bad child, I was warned that I would end up just like her: pregnant, unmarried, who then gave away her child, went to London and went AWOL.

As I was walking out of the hospital, Santa passed me on his way in, carrying a sack of wrapped presents for the sick kids. As I hobbled slowly down Euston Road back to the sin bin of St Pancras it did seem to me that I was now the living embodiment of Aunty Pat. Liked sex too much. "Ruined" because of it.

I got back to the flat, changed into my nightie, wrapped myself in rugs and blankets and sat beside the gas heater that was wafting heady gassy homicidal heat, but heat nonetheless. I sat there, staring into space. I felt really sad. My eye fell on the wee statue Aunty Pat had given me. A tiny, lead, serene cross-legged Buddha. There was a knock at the door. I looked through the peephole, terrified it might be Kieran. It was in fact Nadina, laughing, holding up a bag of potatoes. Nadina, the prostitute who'd previously come begging to my door.

She looked strange through the fisheye lens. I felt a bit apprehensive but opened the door. Nadina thrust the bag into my hands.

"Thanks," I replied.

"Irish people like potatoes, don't they?"

"We like blowing things up as well."

She laughed at the cultural stereotyping. Being London

33

Asian she understood it was like me saying something about *Indians and curries*. She came in and sat down and spotted the pills sitting on the side table.

"What have you got?"

"A miscarriage."

She winced sympathetically.

"I've never had that."

"The bad luck's all mine."

She laughed.

"Heard it's woeful."

"I'll survive." I went back in and rearranged my blankets and rugs around me, repositioning myself nearer the gas fire.

"Do you want some potatoes?" she asked.

I nodded. I started to painstakingly heave myself up from the chair.

"I'll do it."

I wondered if I could trust her in the kitchen, but there really wasn't anything of value to nick, so I nodded. When the spuds were ready, she brought them in on two plates, all smashed up with a fork with a tiny bit of butter on top. In that moment, you know, the spuds were actually the perfect thing. Totally delicious. Especially with the sprinkle of cumin and coriander on top. I was so happy, sitting with her, eating the spuds. She saw Rory's guitar in the corner, beside my fiddle and picked it up. She strummed it, then started to play and to sing softly. I was quite amazed. Her voice was so pure, so real, so deeply and honestly human; heart-wrenching because of the level of anguish and love in her, it made me want to cry. She was singing about someone being a treasure. Simple but beautiful lyrics. With her black wild and matted mane and her pale black skin, her eyes so tightly shut, with the guitar in hands, her head tilting, sinking into the music, it was awesome, primal. I

34

started to realise that this was quite an extraordinary woman. When she finished, I clapped.

"That was brilliant."

"Not bad for a slag," she joked in her husky London accent, taking out her tobacco and skins and rolling herself a cigarette. She stared at the guitar.

"Rory, the guy whose flat this is, owns that, that's mine." I pointed to the fiddle.

"You can't play for a while." She looked at my bandaged hand. I nodded.

"We could start a band. Ladies of the night! What do ya think?" she said with playful glee.

It was a wild idea. But I liked it. "Great name!"

"Lots of creative people live here."

I nodded. They did. Broke ones.

"Where do you live?" I asked.

"Here. Next block." She laughed at what must have been my startled response.

"Who is the treasure you are talking about?" I asked, brushing this over.

"Me," she replied, matter-of-factly.

I felt moved. I wanted to know more but didn't want to pry. Instead, she questioned me. "Your name means 'little flower' in Gaelic."

"How did you know that?"

"You announced it in Burger King when we was all trying to help bandage your bleeding hand."

I laughed, embarrassed, remembering the chaos of the previous night.

"I was really drunk," I said.

"You were really something, not sure if it was drunk, you were wired."

She looked at me, creating the space for me to speak.

"I had met up with my ex."

"Why ex?"

"Well, he is now. He started behaving badly, like with other women, I sort of pretended it wasn't happening. I thought maybe you shouldn't put restrictions on people…"

"Pleasing him, to win him over," she said smiling. I winced inside.

"And then, the other night, in Liverpool, he attacked me while I was sleeping."

She sat up, now listened carefully, with real heart, not phoney or hypocritical heart, or patronising or arrogant heart, or even hard heart, but real heart. She really heard me, which was amazing cos no one else seemed remotely interested.

"Where was he from?"

"Liverpool. Liverpool Irish, parents on both sides from Ireland."

"You thought familiar was safe."

"Yep… I thought he was a bit of a hero, talking up for young kids who get into crime. I thought he was really inspiring. And, of course, the Irish thing…"

"Had he been in prison?"

"Yeah, as a getaway driver for an armed robbery when he was very young."

"But turned bad in prison, a bit of a gangster?"

She was sharp.

"Not quite a gangster."

"Mates with. Probably how he got through prison."

I nodded. "Something like that." I was really only just waking up to all this.

"Anyway, I went to meet him, for a drink, cos he'd said he was sorry."

"Pleasing him," Nadina interrupted. I winced internally again.

"But then it all kind of exploded. I accidentally cut my hand."

She nodded taking it all in.

"What are you going to do in the New Year?"

"I dunno!" I shook my head laughing at the sudden topic change. "Do you know?"

"Probably the same. It's not that bad, Blannie... I'm bidin' my time, bidin' my time, for Richard Gere to show up in his fancy car."

We both laughed hard at that.

"Actually, I wanna get a demo done. Get a record deal. I just have to save a bit of money, then I'm going to live in Greece." She said everything with total confidence, totally convinced in her power. It was dazzling.

"But I dunno if I'd be able to handle the guys in suits, you know from record companies."

"You know how to handle guys."

She smiled, giving me her cheeky grin. "We could both go to Greece, write songs! Then get a demo done. Do it that way round."

I loved her crazy enthusiasm. I told her I didn't really know what I wanted except some structure in my life.

"You're a bit like the Buddha, left his palace on a quest."

I laughed, truly amazed she saw me like that.

"I had a thirst for more life, I dunno, adventure, something to grab me, electrify me, but I grabbed the wrong thing, Nadina. I fell in love with the wrong guy and I dunno maybe now lost my fuckin' mind."

"This is spiritual," she insisted. "Let's see who gets enlightened first."

To see the two of us in our predicament, as if on a spiritual quest, was kind of crazy but also brilliant. She gave it meaning. She gave me hope.

"Do you want to keep hurting yourself, Blathnaid?"

I was startled at her directness.

"He's the one doing the hurting," I replied.

She listened, said nothing, lit her cigarette and inhaled. As she exhaled, the smoke floated through the silence. I caught her eye. There was something in it.

I wanted to know about her. I really did. I was trying to shake off a growing sleepiness. I wanted to listen to her.

Then there was a knock on the door. I jumped, she observed this.

"I'll get it." She got up.

"Thanks."

"I do it for the money," she said casually, reading my mind, as she crossed the room to go and open the door.

I could hear Mike's voice, my neighbour from downstairs.

"Is Blathnaid in? I was wonderin' if I could borrow a cup of sugar from her."

Rory had told me all about him in advance. Mike was from Dublin and a junkie. But he had a good soul and someone not to be scared of. I had been a bit scared of him, but by now I knew Mike was alright.

"Yes, that's fine," I called out to him.

I got up from my seat and hobbled down the corridor to get the sugar for him.

"Are you okay?" Mike asked. "I saw you the other night."

"Yeah, yeah," I said.

Mike stood there in his black canvas trousers, far too skinny, with his eyes peering out behind his strange pink-tinted glasses. They made his eyes look a touch pink also. Made me think of a sick rabbit. He had jet black hair and a very strong Dublin accent. Mike handed me his cup for the sugar.

"Any news from Rory?"

"No, nothing, still travelling."

Mike was on methadone. He must have been the only junkie in the world who had never stolen, hard to believe, I know, but the god's honest truth. He was so bloody soft, the only thing he had ever damaged was himself. He was also profoundly intelligent. Very curious about people. I had some quite interesting chats with him about *Ulysses*. There is no doubt the Dublin working class are the most cultured in the world. And so polite also, always so courteous. Well, *he* was.

"This is Nadina," I said.

As I went into the kitchen to get the sugar, I could hear him talking to Nadina about Hindu gods, Shiva and Krishna, and about how he'd read in Hindu mythology that life in the world was maintained by Krishna's breathing. I liked the idea of the earth being inside this nice-looking Asian guy's lungs, expanding and contracting as he breathed in and out.

"What do you do?" I heard Mike ask Nadina.

"Hand jobs for a tenner."

He laughed, clearly liking her spirit.

"I heard you singing, I thought you were a singer."

I joined them at the door and handed Mike the cup with sugar. I was now one of them. Outcasts, dregs of society. But in my eyes, in that moment, we were little urban shamans, not ruined or broken or even that hardened. People of humanity – which, as I increasingly realised, was so fuckin' rare, anywhere. In that moment, I loved them both.

"You not going home then for Christmas?" asked Mike.

"No."

"Well, happy Christmas to you, Blathnaid."

"Thanks, happy Christmas to you, Mike."

"And to you, Nadina," Mike added.

Nadina laughed sardonically. "Happy Christmas one and all."

After they left, I made myself a cup of tea and sat down again by the heater. I could hear Mike downstairs playing *Velvet Underground* and then talking to his dad on the phone and crying. He was telling him he loved him over and over. It was God awful to hear. I put on an Etta James tape to block it out and lay down on the sofa to rest. She was singing about a merry Christmas and receiving a diamond ring and how she was in paradise, which for some reason made me laugh. I thought about Kieran, meeting him, in the bar where they played trad Irish music, the instant attraction, the good-natured banter. The feeling for him hadn't disappeared. It was shoved aside by the terror and confusion from his recent attack. I must have fallen asleep on the sofa.

I had a horrible dream about crawling around on my hands and knees searching for a baby in a room full of children. I was in a bathroom, watching fluid go down a plughole. I didn't want it to go down. Then there was the sound of really loud crashing in my dream.

I woke up, shell-shocked to see Kieran standing in the doorway, staring at me. I screamed. I thought maybe I was still dreaming. But he was real.

"It's okay. I just want to talk to you... get up and we'll have a cup of tea and a chat."

I nodded. His light chit-chat felt surreal.

As I got up, I saw that the front door had been kicked open and a guy, with his back to me, was standing at the unlit entrance. I turned to ask Kieran what was going on, when he hit me across the face with such force I went flying across the room, hitting the side of my cheek against the heavy wood junk table that the TV was on. Dazed, I tried to get up to run out of the already blocked exit. But he pushed me down again and then crouching, put his hands round my neck area, sort of throttling me, banging the back of my head against the solid table. His mouth a line thin and the whites of his eyes widened. He looked crazy. I thought this was definitely death.

"Don't you fuckin' DARE speak to me like that in front of people... do you hear me? STUPID bitch."

He got up to go, then turned to kick me one more time. I felt a surge of rage. Red-hot rage streaming out of me. Adrenalin pumping, I grabbed his ankle, jerked it. I heard myself roaring, screaming. He lost his balance, landed on the floor, crashing his head. It didn't split or anything. I stared, shocked. Suddenly male arms were grabbing me, yanking me backwards. Must have been the guy at the door. I was trying to resist, kicking. Kieran, whose eyes were shut, was breathing. I twisted my head, to see who was holding me. It was his friend Nick, from Newry, who used to be in the IRA. I had mostly only met Kieran with his trendy mates and only dipped into his other reality a few times. More pounding noise, as two policemen came rushing into my sitting room. They asked what had happened? I didn't say anything. I couldn't say anything. I couldn't speak. I should have but I just couldn't. Kieran got up from the floor. One of the policemen said something about bickering micks.

"Whose flat is it?"

"Mine."

"Your name?"

"Blathnaid O' Sullivan."

"Yours?"

"Kieran Flaherty."

"And you are? Paddy Mick O'Murphy or something?" The policemen laughed.

"Nick Murray. Close."

"What's going on?"

None of us said anything.

"You two are coming with us."

This was addressed to Kieran and Nick who nodded, strangely without protest. The policeman then told me to come down to the station in the morning to make a statement; said I also needed to get the door fixed. Just like that it was all over.

I watched them out of the window, down on the street, with the blue light of the police car flashing, I could see them putting Kieran and Nick in the car.

I sat down on the sofa, dazed. I lit a cigarette and then another one, hands shaking. As the adrenalin wore off, I thought I might boke. I wondered who'd phoned the police. I looked at the broken open door. Anyone could come in. The tiny lead Buddha that Aunty Pat had given me caught my eye again. I didn't really like her the few times I met her but I thought the statue was beautiful. I put it in my pocket.

I crept down the stairwell in the dark and stopped outside David's flat. I knocked on his door, he didn't answer. I knocked again, waited and was about to give up when the door opened.

"I'm on holiday abroad in a hot country."

"Someone broke into my flat, they've been arrested. But the door is broken... could I stay the night?"

It wasn't an easy thing to ask. His brown eyes were wary. It wasn't an immediate yes. He looked at my face which stung and was really grazed. He nodded and I followed him inside.

"Want a cup of tea?"

"Yes, please."

"Milk and sugar?"

"Yes, just one sugar. Actually two."

"I can make it three if you like"

I sank down on the dark red sofa in his sitting room while

42

David went into the kitchen. I was amazed how well he'd done up his flat. It was practically luxurious in comparison to mine. Still squatty but sanded wooden floor, white painted walls, wooden box used as a coffee table, with two huge comfy shabby chic sofas in a right angle facing a television. There were also some beautiful photographs of Africa on the wall.

He handed me a mug of tea.

"You do have a thing with the emergency services. Ambulance. Police. Got plans for the fire brigade?"

I laughed.

"'Course you're used to that, what with the paras breaking down your door on a nightly basis. Living on the Falls Road, dodging the bullets. Standing in the rain at all those IRA funerals. In your black beret."

"I didn't live on the Falls Road."

He smiled, nodding. He'd sussed that.

"What's going on? Is there some kind of axe murderer chasing you?"

"More like a psycho ex-boyfriend," I said as lightly as I could.

I noticed the poster of 'Leatherhead' from the slasher film *The Texas Chainsaw Massacre* on his wall. He clearly saw violence with an unreal film lens. He got up and went into another room and came out with some tissues and a tube of Savlon.

"You need to get an injunction, or go to a woman's refuge if you need a safe space."

The term 'women's refuge' hit like a brick. I was in battered wife territory. Fuck. That's how he saw me. Fuck. That was a terrible place to be. Also, this stay was clearly just for the evening. Emergency aid. Of course, he was right, we didn't know each other.

"I'm going to go back to Belfast day after Boxing Day. Banks are open then."

"What so you can rob one?"

He was a sarky fucker, but this time I did smile.

"So a cheque will have cleared by then."

"You're welcome to stay till then."

"Seriously, thank you."

"How 'seriously' dangerous is this guy?"

I didn't want to scare him. Truth is I didn't know.

"He doesn't know I'm here."

"You're welcome to stay."

I caught his eye. This was huge of him. I felt exhausted. I could also now feel a throbbing pain in my cheek.

"I'm knackered."

He nodded.

"I'll show you the spare room."

I got up as he did and followed him, pointing out the bathroom and toilet on the way.

"Feel free to use the towels. I've just done a wash. So all clean."

He pointed to one towel in particular. I nodded. We carried on to the end of the passage. He opened the door. It was a little awkward and he was being formal to make it easier. I walked into his tiny spare room with a single bed and shelf with books on it. There were white walls and like a Mexican rug as a bed throw in vibrant bright yellow and red colours, a chair and a small mirror on the wall. He looked at me and smiled. He was still carrying the tissues and Savlon and handed them to me.

"Thanks. That rug Mexican?"

He nodded.

"Beautiful."

He went to go but stopped at the door. "Are you okay?"

The compassionate gaze in his eyes pierced me, it was so different to his earlier dry, detached tone. I couldn't really answer but I felt an overwhelming urge to nestle into him. It was purely instinctual as really he was practically a stranger.

He left. I closed the door. I looked at my face in the mirror. Jesus. I looked a fuckin' wreck. My gelled-up hair, sort of fluffy punky look was all flat. The side of my face was red, bright red near my eye. My black eyeliner looked wrong with the redness. I put a bit of the Savlon on my cheek. I lay down on the bed. I fell asleep in my clothes. Incredibly… I slept.

I dreamt of a woman. She was being attacked by a man. She called out and a raging pack of dogs appeared. The man, who then somehow had a stag's head on him, fled, the dogs raced after him, hunting him. They caught up with him, attacking him viciously in a frenzy. Life went out of the man with the stag's head. The woman appeared with a bow and arrow, the dogs gathered round her. Smiling, she shot an arrow into the sky.

The bedroom door opened. I woke, screamed. It was David, standing at the door in a red and white Santa hat. When I realised it was him, we both laughed in a kind of freaked-out kind of way.

"Happy Christmas!"

"Jesus Christ, you scared the shit out of me."

"So I did." He mimicked my accent.

"Don't," I said not liking the mimicking. He laughed.

"I'm going round to my parents."

"I'm going to the police to press charges."

"Today? Christmas Day?"

I nodded.

"Well, help yourself to coffee and toast. There is a fresh pot. No turkey, I'm afraid."

"Coffee and toast are wonderful." I smiled.

"Spare key is on the table. See you later."

I nodded. "Thanks."

After breakfast, I walked down the side alley on my way to the police. It was deadly quiet. A woman with SAVED

45

handwritten on her forehead walked towards me. She was wearing a denim mini skirt, high heels and was drunk or off her face on something.

She walked past singing, "Oh Happy Day."

I was thinking of a witty quip.

"Blathnaid." It was a Northern Irish accent.

I turned. Walking towards me was Nick, the ex-IRA guy who'd broken into my flat with Kieran. I could smell a dirty rat coming. I felt like a really tight pressure against my skin as if it was stretched too tightly. He stopped in front of me.

"The peelers aren't following this up."

"What?"

"Kieran has decided not to press charges."

"What? What are you talking about?"

"He's not goin' to press charges."

I looked at him utterly incredulous.

"They've been let off with a police caution and the police have promised to keep a close eye on them. So, you're safe."

"Keep a close eye on who?"

"That Paki brasser you've been hangin' out with and her pimp fella."

My jaw dropped. They were pinning this on Nadina and her pimp. How the hell did they make the connection between me and Nadina? So clearly their line was Kieran had rescued me from King Cross scum who were breaking in and got roughed up in the process, but wasn't pressing charges. Nadina and pimp would also know whatever they say will not be believed, that's if they knew at all. An injunction needs police paperwork, and an intimidating 'ex' IRA guy was telling me all this. Basically, I was totally fucking snookered.

Nick looked at the marks on my face.

"I didn't realise they attacked you as well."

"Wise up, Kieran did that. As you know."

46

A stare between us. He took out some money.

"How much for the door?"

"Fuck off."

He kind of laughed. A hard dry laugh.

I walked off. This was getting really scary. I walked around the block a couple of times, my mind buzzing on overload. I carried on walking and walking quickly and even quicker, round the block a few times more and found myself in the next courtyard, walking up the steps to Yoichi's flat. I had no appointment booked and it was Christmas Day. But I knocked anyway and Yoichi opened the door, more than a touch surprised when he saw me. Nevertheless, he gestured to me to come in. I walked inside. A woman in her late twenties was chanting to the scroll that Yoichi had hanging in his wooden cabinet. I sat down; a bit weirded out. I looked at the Buddhist scroll. It had bold black Chinese or Japanese characters written down the centre and smaller writing on either side. It was beautiful. Fresh.

"She'll finish soon," he told me.

Yoichi sat behind her and chanted with her. My squashed-up mind, kind of expanded just listening to them. And then, out of curiosity, I picked up the words and murmured the mantra with them. There was a lovely moment when the winter sun rays came in through the window and lit us all. It was like we were in deep harmony with all and each other.

After a while I felt my mind relax, the tight clench of anxiety, fear and hopeless rage loosened its grip. I felt space in my head that was free. I felt and found a state of happiness in my mind. Hard to explain. I had this happiness in me, tucked away, buried beneath the current relentless terror treadmill. It was a bit like being high on dope, like that little pocket of happiness you hit. But this was natural, legal. A loving feeling to everything. I could see me and what was happening and my heart opened to me. I felt a real compassion to me. I just felt I didn't want my own life hurt anymore. This was a warm, loving, spacious feeling. Not tight. Goodness had not left my world. And I wanted to give that goodness also. It was class.

The woman finished chanting and turned round to look at me. She was smiling and had such an 'alive' vibrant presence; I could feel her energy. She looked Italian.

"I got here late to see Yoichi, maybe it meant we could meet on time!"

I laughed. "Divine timing!"

She smiled.

"I support the young women locally, what happened your face?"

"Psycho ex-boyfriend," I joked. I did a cartoon-like mock punch to my face.

She laughed, liking my black humour.

"Did you walk into a wall?" she asked. I realised she hadn't quite taken it in.

"No. Actually him or his mate kicked the door in."

She didn't laugh this time. "I'm Rita."

I nodded. I liked her Italian accent.

"What's your name?"

"Blathnaid. Means 'little flower'.."

"Out of the muddy swamp the Lotus flower blooms."

"So, we can get out of the swamp of Kings Cross?" I said joking.

"We can get out of our lowest life state, bring out our Buddha state."

"Yeah, I think I felt it… beautiful."

I looked at Yoichi. He was putting mince pies on a plate. He had his silver Christmas tree with fairy lights on in the corner. It was bonkers; he had way more Christmas decorations than anyone else's flat I'd been in.

"Happiness not holiness."

Yoichi clapped his hands in delight. I'd got it.

"Happiness in you, all time. *And* can get out of the Kings Cross, anytime!" Yoichi said this with a warm smile. He had such clear joyful eyes. He offered me a mince pie. I took it.

"What do you do, Yoichi?"

"I work in a sushi restaurant on Eversholt Street."

I nodded. Yoichi could see my fascination.

In my mind, Buddhas, were eastern male monks in orange robes who meditated in hill-top monasteries. I thanked them both and left. I felt a lot better. A lot clearer too. Outside it was snowing. Kind of magical Christmas Day stuff. But as I was walking through the courtyard, my heart seized up as, through the falling snow, I saw Kieran walking towards me. He stopped, casually blocking my path. There were some picnic tables in the courtyard, so I indicated we sit there. I wanted to stay in public. I could smell the booze off him.

"Your mate Mike told me you had a miscarriage."

So it was Mike. He was the one who told Kieran about Nadina also. Probably rang the police as well.

"When did you speak to Mike?"

"Last night, I came back, to see if you were okay."

I felt sick. This was enough. I'd had enough.

"You weren't there."

I shook my head. Careful not to say a word.

"I didn't know you were pregnant. You didn't tell me… why didn't you tell me?"

"I wasn't hundred percent aware of it myself. Very early on. But I thought I did say."

He looked at me, with a hint of concern.

"I'm going to rent a place for the New Year in Brighton. You could come and stay for a few days. Rest."

I shook my head. "It's enough."

I took out the little lead Buddha that Aunty Pat had

given to me; it was still in my pocket from the previous night. I stared at it. I wanted that peace. I leant across and gave it to him. The attachment, the invisible chord whatever it was tying us, snapped.

He picked it up, looked at it carelessly, then got the seriousness of my gaze. Then I walked away. He called my name once, but not twice. Maybe he felt it was enough also, but, to be honest, I was still fearful I might hear his footsteps behind me.

I kept on walking. I looked round a few times, to check, but he wasn't behind me. I felt strong. Kind of exhilarated. I'd changed. Maybe I'd even changed my karma. It was still snowing. But I didn't feel any cold. I kept walking all the way to Covent Garden. No one was around. The shops were closed. I found myself a quiet spot in Neal's Yard, under a droopy snowy tree. This had been a shit Christmas but I forced myself to think about next year, the future.

On the way back, I was still mulling everything over, what I was going to do, how I would do it, until I reached the top of Midhope Street, when I saw police and tape and an ambulance outside the building I lived in. Someone was screaming. The girlfriend of the New Zealand artist appeared out of the building, hysterical. Horrified, I then watched as Mike was taken out.

He looked dead.

But nothing prepared me for what I saw next.

Everything went into slow motion as I witnessed Kieran carried out on a stretcher, bright red blood splattered across his white shirt. He looked dead also. I stared; not able to let what I saw connect to the reality of what it was. I became vaguely aware of David running towards me. Everything was muffled. Kieran, he said, had been stabbed multiple times with a broken bottle.

David told the police I lived there and they let me through.

I went back to David's in a daze. We sat, unable to speak. My mind was jangled, jumbled.

I looked at David; he was really jangled also.

"What thoughts are going on underneath that elusive surface?"

"Just glad it wasn't the other way round," he replied.

It was still snowing softly outside.

I thought about the little statue.

I thought about Aunty Pat. I wondered if maybe she wasn't so bad.

There was a knock on the door. "Police."

David opened the door. Two policemen walked inside. They interviewed us quickly, and left. It came on the news as they were going. A man seriously injured in a stabbing incident in Kings Cross. Another man dead from a drug overdose. The implication was that one had tried to kill the other then killed himself. A druggy seasonal brawl that had got out of control.

But I sensed it was more than that.

I cried.

I also felt a colossal relief.

I could breathe.

For now… released.

David heated up some plum pudding he'd brought back from his mum's.

We ate it silently and watched *White Christmas*, with Bing Crosby, on TV.

Part III

Nadina

It was Boxing Day. Most of the snow had gone. I left David's just after breakfast to post a late Christmas card to my sister, when I bumped into Nadina.

She was standing on her own near the post office, in a mini skirt and high heels. No one was really about. She walked back with me as I was still a bit shaky on my feet. Mainly from the miscarriage but everything that had happened had mad-wobbled me for sure. We went and sat in Argyle Square, it didn't feel right to bring her into David's flat, he was still sheltering me, so I didn't want to take the piss. It was a clear chilly wintry day as we sat on the park bench, surrounded by the huge trees, puffing our fags. I realised we were becoming kind of friends. And seeing as mine were thin on the ground, I appreciated it. I was telling her about everything as she didn't know anything.

She didn't know she and her pimp had been blamed for breaking in to my flat.

Or that Mike was dead. From a heroin overdose.

Or Kieran, my violent ex, was in hospital from being lunged at by a broken bottle.

She blinked in surprise. I joked that I was the BBC Newsflash.

Kings Cross was a village, a sick village, but a village none the less. There was a genuine community as well as genuine mayhem. Some of the kids were out playing football and some winos on another bench. One of the older winos started slowly filtering through the rubbish bin. It was tough to watch. A young girl emerged out of the bushes, and was given cash from a guy, presumably payment. I was shocked but hid it. She started walking towards us. I vaguely recognised her as one of the prostitutes from the post office. She was young, sixteen, maybe seventeen max.

Nadina waved at her. She waved back.

"Where you goin', Abbie?"

She stopped. It was strange being so close to this kind of conversation.

"I have a meeting. We're gonna do the occupation," Abbie said.

"What? You mean my idea?" Nadina was laughing.

"What occupation?" I asked.

"We're bein' harassed by the police, it's getting out of control," replied Nadina. "We're going to occupy the church."

"The church? Around the corner?"

Nadina nodded. "Hookers in the house."

"Hookers in the house," I said picking up the rhythm.

"Hookers in the house of—" She looked to me to finish our spontaneous rap.

"Lords!" I said. She clicked her fingers, smiling in delight.

"Could be of the Lord," she mused.

"Nads, have you 50p or any spare fags?" asked Abbie.

Nadina took out her ten deck and gave her two.

"I'm going round to the women's centre to talk with Susan."

Nadina nodded. "She knows what I think."

"What's the women's centre?" I asked gripped by all this.

"ECP: English Collective of Prostitutes," she replied.

Nadina told Abbie that she would catch her later. Abbie left.

Nadina then suggested we go skating to the outside ice rink on The Strand.

"What? No way. I can't skate! I'm supposed to be resting."

"You can rest on your feet. Come on. I love skating."

"What are you goin' to skate in?"

"My knickers. They give you skates there."

I laughed at her *fuck it, devil-may-care* attitude. I kind of got caught up with it and went along with it. A police car crawled alongside us on the way and gave Nadina gip. One of them called her a dirty Paki. But she mostly ignored it, until they got bored and drove away.

When we got there, the sun was out. All the old buildings looked majestic. I remember noticing again the beautiful light blue of the winter sky. It soothed my eyes. So did the pure white of the ice rink. It was huge. I watched Nadina skating, from behind the barrier. She was with all the other people, gliding up and then past me, waving and smiling at me with that look of glee in her eyes. It was nice to watch. And hilarious when she was playing at slipping on the ice and then really did fall on her ass.

I didn't have her bravery. I wasn't ready to immerse myself in anything yet.

A bit of my brain passed out the night of Kieran's attack, I was still coming round. Still trying to process what happened. What do you call that? Was that rape? I thought that was something that happened walking home late at night, not what your sort of boyfriend did while you lie asleep in bed. I shut my eyes and tried to transport myself to a holiday, lying on a soft sandy beach under a blazing hot sun. I felt a shake. It was Nadina at the other side of the barrier.

"Wake up, Blannie, you dreamin'?"

"Yes. Of a continental holiday."

"Ah yeah, I'd like that, in Greece. With a little donkey," Nadina said.

"A little donkey?"

"Yeah. I'll learn to ride it on the beach."

This made me laugh.

"Why a little donkey and not a sleek big chic horse?"

"Cos I'd like a little donkey," she said with utter certainty and an impish glee.

"It's my continental holiday!"

She laughed and skated off again, she looked so free and happy. She then got out and came and joined me with others watching from the side of the rink.

"I know nothing about you," I said.

She looked at me and smiled, but with an intense look in her direct, deep stare, which still gave nothing away.

"What do you want to know? How I got on the game?"

I didn't say anything, because of course I did. But I felt ashamed at my curiosity.

"I'm from Brixton, both my parents Indian. My father was at me from when I was about four. My mum didn't 'see' it. When I was a bit older, I told a teacher at school. My dad was arrested. He pleaded guilty, went to prison. Justice. But then in prison he killed himself. I had a nervous breakdown. All my mates legged it. Like yours."

"No they haven't. It's Christmas," I protested. Nadina gave me a look.

"I was shoved into a mental hospital, diagnosed with manic depression. My family and I dumped each other. Towards the end in the mental hospital, I took myself off lithium, without them knowing. I didn't want to be a lobotomised dribbling cabbage anymore. Know what I mean?"

I tried to not show on my face how shocking this all was to hear. I nodded. The side of the skating rink felt a strange place to tell me all this, but she was like that. Didn't hold back.

"I'd crashed. I was gonna go to art school, actually. I can hardly believe that now, you know, with a wham bam nervous breakdown. Just one of those things, you know. I suppose having it off with your dad, crude, I know, does your nut in. Especially then when he goes and kills himself. The catch about telling people is that, on the one hand it's like the truth, you know? But then on the other hand, it like puts you in victim mode, well, in freak mode actually, 'cause let's face it, it is a pretty weird thing. I mean it's not normal. I can understand why people turn round and look at me appalled. I would too if it wasn't me. If I were to meet me and by chance be told it, I think I'd probably want to totally avoid me. Know what I mean?"

I laughed. The way she said it had ended up being funny.

"Am I looking suitably appalled?"

She laughed, relieved. She visibly relaxed.

"People can outlive their own tragedy, you know, Blan. We both have splinters in our souls which we're extracting. To the normal people we're losers, but we're both dealing with the undealable in some way, and coming out of it enlightened."

She had been talking non-stop without a break. Like it was pouring out of her. Like she needed to say it. This thing about becoming enlightened was so important to her. Made it all worthwhile. I liked that. It made it all more than a fall down from the bad man.

She was a romantic at heart. I guess so was I.

"I still haven't told you how I got on the game," she said teasing a little.

I shrugged. "It's kind of obvious."

She laughed lightly, a little hollowly. A young girl fell over on the ice, looked like she might cry but then got up, was helped up.

56

"Why don't we go to Greece, for a couple of weeks, write songs?"

I nodded. It could be nice. She had said that before, sort of as a joke, but this time I felt it was serious. I took it seriously now too.

"That's what the Mamas and Papas did before they got their deal."

"I wouldn't ever be a junkie, Blathnaid. I've taken smack a couple of times but not my bag. I want a clear head. I hate being foggy."

I must have looked unconvinced about something as she launched into a mighty verbal counter-attack.

"Blan, I'm independent! My mum was shoved into an arranged marriage; she'd met my dad once. Once! Never had any control. I have money. I've never been beaten up by a punter. Never. Fucking men, only way to deal with them, is to make them pay. In all ways."

I laughed at her might. She had such power in her delivery.

"What about the guy who looks after you? He was shouting at you the day you came up to my flat. Looking for money."

She stopped as if briefly caught out.

"The punter hadn't given me the full amount. I blew up at Steve 'cos I was telling him the truth and he didn't believe me. Steve's a dick, yeah, but he's alright. He doesn't really look after me, it's a very loose thing, not what you think."

I was amazed by her and also her incredible humanity. She was powerful. I believed in her entirely.

"Fear is the opposite to love. Nothing will work in your life, Blannie, until you love yourself."

She looked up at the sun in the sky against the crisp light blue winter sky.

"I used to look at the sun rising and imagine I was in love, to make myself feel better, still do. I looked at the blueness of the sky also, you have to sense the sky is part of you. You're beautiful too. That's how I got myself off lithium."

I listened quite amazed by her strength. She was able to give, really give, without looking for return. There was no sense of a 'deal', she could be aloof, rude to people she didn't like. But she had no shame, she had no doubt about herself and she was open to learning. She had a kind of infectious optimism too.

Walking on Sunshine by Katrina and The Waves started playing on a gay guy's portable radio standing near us, also watching the skaters. Nadina started dancing to it. She shut her eyes and swayed, moving her arms up and down, stamping, a wildness in her, mirth erupting to her lips. The gay guys whistled and watched and one joined in dancing, arms in the air. I suddenly got a burst of joy and energy and joined in the dancing too, clicking my hand to the beat, moving my arms and hips in unison. And for a moment at the side of the ice rink, we were all 'Walking on Sunshine'.

The next day I called round to Nadina's flat which was really quite basic, just one room, in the next courtyard. She made a point of saying she never worked from there. We had a cup of tea and some aloo paratha, Indian potato bread, that she had made, flour and water and spuds, a bit like Northern Irish potato bread and then we walked into Covent Garden.

I loved it there, I was enchanted by the artistic shop displays, made out of branches and stones. And the little lit Lotus candles floating in water bowls with multi-coloured glass pebbles glistening inside. It was like walking from hell to heaven, and it only took half an hour.

All the Christmas lights were still up. So, it was extra magic. We walked into an ethnicy shop called The Eastern

Store. It was laden with a strange mixture of the very expensive and the very cheap. It had all these beautiful eastern rugs and fabrics hanging from the walls, heavy cloths: dark burgundy with silk golden threads, deep crimson fabrics, and indigo Chinese jackets also. There were also blue and white porcelain china bowls lined up alongside cheap Chinese lampshades hanging from the walls. Bonsai plants, woks, African masks, basically everything you can imagine that was vaguely eastern, or ethnic, all crammed in together. There was a kind of wonderful equality about that cramming. And it worked, all merged beautifully together.

Nadina wrapped one of the expensive throws with golden threads around her, covering everything except her eyes. She stared at me, her intense non-pleasing, deep stare. She looked good. She knew it. A sales assistant came marching towards us. We legged it.

We went across the road into a shop that sold designer rave clothes and I tried on an expensive designer silver bubble jacket and funky smiley culture hat. We pissed ourselves laughing and left again just as the manager approached. We then wandered slowly into Neal's Yard where I had gone on Christmas Day. The decorations were still up and the shops now open and people were eating this lovely food outside: salads with walnuts and raisins. It was like a little paradise, people sitting chatting under the same tree, I'd sat under. Some had nice expensive brown camel coats on. I noticed the quality of the coats. The look of wealth became fresh again to my eye. There was a tea shop, with lots of different types of tea and Japanese-looking teapots. It had a big picture of a fat laughing Buddha in the window.

We sat down and had a pot of green tea which seemed both exotic and extravagant.

I showed Nadina a photo of Kieran I still had in my bag.

"He's in intensive care."

"You still have a photo of him?"

She was right, it was weird. She took it off me and stared at it.

I went to take the photo off her but she held onto it. It kind of creeped me out.

"Give it to me!"

"Don't grab!"

I scrunched it up and threw it in the nearby bin proving my strength. There was awkwardness. Our first little tiff. She stared at her green tea morosely.

The people sitting nearby were talking about a rally against the government, some bill that was becoming law in the New Year. It was all happening in Trafalgar Square. They had just come from there and said there were thousands of people. It sounded exciting and I thought it was a good way to get past the weird moment.

"Shall we go and have a look?"

"At the rally?"

"Yeah, why not?"

"I like it here."

"Come on."

"I don't want to," she insisted stubbornly, still drinking her green tea.

"We can come back after, just have a look."

"Okay." She got up reluctantly.

When we got to the bottom of Charing Cross Road and curved round into Trafalgar Square with the National Gallery at the back of it and the statue of Admiral Nelson at the centre, it was literally crammed with thousands of people. It took us both by surprise, we didn't expect so many. There was a deafening noise, from people screaming and shouting and holding placards. Some people were chanting anti-Thatcher chants. For a split second as we stood there on the side, it felt positively powerful. Change creating. But then the skirmishes started to break out beside us. The whole thing escalated really quickly. My Belfast antennae went up. I could feel it was getting nasty. Loads of police on horses arrived, coming down the street behind us, blocking our way out. One was holding a loudspeaker; he was telling the crowd to disperse and warning us of the consequences. I turned to Nadina. She widened her eyes, alarmed.

"Effectively he's just read us The Riot Act," I said.

"What does that mean?"

"It means we have to get the fuck out of here."

And indeed, there was an immense charge from a whole line of police on horses spreading the full width of the road and at full gallop right into the crowd. It was terrifying. The sound of the screaming was thunderous. The pavements were practically shaking as people ran away or fought with police on the ground. One guy was being torn between the police and some of the protestors; they were both pulling at either side of his body and his clothes were being pulled off in the struggle. He was totally limp; he may have been unconscious. There was a woman beside him screaming right in the face of the police. It was animalistic and raw and totally out of control. I could see an overturned car burning not far away. I looked at Nadina and indicated to the road opposite, still unblocked. She nodded.

Without speaking we ran like fury towards Piccadilly. But the road was now blocked and the protestors were now throwing their placards at the police. More police had appeared with full riot gear on, baton shields and batons, and they were running, charging en masse, beating people. A police Saracen drove at full speed down towards us right into the crowd. We jumped out of the way. It was fucking full on.

61

Looking at each other, with mounting panic, we turned back the way we had come, kept running, running, terrified. Luckily, I spotted a narrow bit of the path on the same side as the National Gallery that was still unblocked. We ran through it and up Charing Cross Road as if our lives depended on it. When we were in the clear, we stopped, out of breath.

"Last bloody time I'll listen to any of your bright ideas," quipped Nadina.

"How was I to know?"

She looked at me, rolling her eyes, laughing.

"Come on," Nadina said. "Let's get out of here."

Some casual looting was going on as some of the shop windows had been broken. Nadina ran across and quickly grabbed a toaster.

Exhilarated by the lawless spirit, I followed suit and nabbed a hairdryer. When we saw police on horses in the distance, heading in our direction we ran, cutting down a pedestrian side street into Covent Garden.

We stopped, panting again, out of breath. I sat down on a nearby wall. Nadina sat down beside me.

"I stabbed him."

I felt the blood drain from my face.

"What?"

"Kieran. I stabbed him." She shut her eyes and, tilting her head to the side, slowly glided towards me, as if to kiss. I moved my head away. She opened her eyes.

"Blathnaid!"

A familiar voice. I turned to see Ava, standing, holding shopping bags.

Two worlds crashed.

Ava looked at Nadina. Her face did not register any kind of expression but I could see a kind of lightning-fast glimmer at the back of her eyes as she took in Nadina.

"Ava!" I immediately got up. As if I had been caught out somehow.

I hugged her. She hugged me back.

"Blathnaid!"

Ava had a face which was empathetic but very good at concealing her thoughts.

"This is my friend Nadina."

Ava turned and smiled politely, even quite warmly at her.

"Hi."

Nadina looked blank and barely looked at Ava. There was a sense of latent hostility. I quickly glanced at Nadina. She got up.

"Have to go."

As she was crossing the road, she turned.

It was the way she looked at me.

A shiver went through me, as I watched her reach the other side and disappear into the crowd.

"What was that about?" asked Ava.

"She had to go." Ava looked at me. Her eyes practically glinting now.

Of course, that was not what her question meant but she didn't press it any further.

"Still on for my hen night next week?"

"Of course."

I really didn't feel up to it. But there was no way I wouldn't go.

"Still up for playing something at the wedding?"

This did feel too hard.

"I dunno, if… I don't know if I can really…"

I gestured to my still bandaged hand. Ava glared.

"I've written a poem. Could I read a poem instead?"

Ava paused, unsure.

"Can I hear it?"

"I think I can remember it."

"Go on then." She looked at me with an expectant smile in her eyes. I started.

"This is for the dregs, the outcasts, the underdogs, the misfits, the mongrels and the abused.

For the unemployed, the underpaid, the underclass, the Giro Generation..."

"Stop!" Ava demanded.

"The powerless, the poor, the E takers, anti D takers I—"

"STOP."

Ava held up her hand. Her face was drawn so tight I thought it would crack. Her shrewd blue eyes now glared with fury.

"It's a wedding." She practically spat out the words. I tried to backtrack.

"I was just giving you a taster. Something meaningful."

"Meaningful for a wedding!"

"Yes. Yes. It will be."

"I need to read it first."

"Of course."

"Are you alright?" Ava asked.

"I phoned you," I replied.

"Yes, I'm sorry. I wasn't able to get back. I'm just snowed under."

"He raped me, Ava."

"Well, you deserve what you get, running around in miniskirts, up drinking and partying half the night."

I was stung by the biting judgement. Had she heard me? I had forgotten about that twisted sister shit; that strange hug you at the front, stab you at the back, but sometimes take the knife out of your back also, help bandage you. It was a very strange complex dance. Might have been easier

64

to be a guy and have a punch-up in the street and a make up in the bar.

"I had a miscarriage. Very early."

Immediate regret showed on Ava's face.

"You can come and stay with us for a couple of nights if that helps."

"Thanks. The troubling person is gone... so."

She blinked. Not understanding and not wanting to. It was too much. She couldn't handle it. She was about to get married. Me/this she did not need.

"I have to go... I have a fitting."

I nodded. Strangely gutted she hadn't asked me to go to the fitting with her.

"See you next week. I hope the fitting goes well."

She nodded and sort of smiled.

She hovered for a moment, we stared at each other.

She kissed me briskly on the cheek.

"Is that girl a prostitute?"

I shook my head. "No."

"I'll phone you."

I nodded. "Thanks."

I watched her go. I felt kind of sad.

As I walked back, to Kings Cross, my head spun.

I thought of Nadina, and what she had said.

I walked into The Boot, a pub on Cromer that had reopened. I had enough for a half pint. As I was turning around from the bar, who did I see, in the corner with a big fat smile and a big fat pint in front of him? Yoichi. He smiled, raised his glass to me.

It was an old geezers' pub basically. Dark inside. Sparse. Worn out patterned carpet. An ol' straggly Christmas tree with emaciated silver tinsel in the corner. I got a half pint and walked over to Yoichi.

"Having a nice Christmas?"

"I'm drowning my sorrows."

"Drink won't make it better.

"Temporarily it will."

He glanced at my puny skinny half pint.

"Well, you'll need more than that."

"Too right."

His eyes shone. He loved my backchat.

"What you angry about?"

"Nadina."

"I don't know her."

"She lives or rather 'works' around here."

He immediately got what I was saying.

"I thought she was like a kind of mystic but she's maybe she's just a talented gobshite."

"Maybe. But power in you," he said.

"WHAT ARE YOU TALKING ABOUT? THERE IS NO POWER IN ME."

Silence. I gathered myself and took a sip. So did he.

I noticed he was calm, my outburst had bounced off him.

"How long have you been in London?"

"Long time. Since I got married. I worked as porter in hospital, then get job in Japanese restaurant, washing dishes then studied from a cook then graduated to cook, small place, I like it."

"I didn't know you were married."

"She dead. Cancer... Akkiko."

He said it matter-of-factly but I could see the mention brought sadness. It was a deep, private pain.

A guy came in to the bar, tubby-looking guy.

"Yoichi!"

Yoichi smiled. He came over.

"What'll you have?" he asked.

Yoichi pointed to his pint glass.

"Same again. Stout."

"What my wife always says!"

Yoichi and I both laughed.

The guy looked at me to see if I wanted one.

"No. Thanks. Just going."

Yoichi smiled at me as I drained my puny half pint. I was a disgrace to the hard drinkers of my nation. Maybe Nadina was just a bullshitter. Buoyed up by the half pint and the comradery, I felt ready for the world again. I went through Yoichi's courtyard as a shortcut to David's. The sun was setting. St Pancras' spire could be seen. I went up the stairwell for a few flights to look at it from the roof top.

I felt strangely hungry. I had an intense desire to put something in my mouth. Nuts, Bombay mix, gum, anything. The half pint comradery was wearing off. Had Nadina stabbed Kieran? Jesus, this was insane. My head was spinning again. What the hell was I supposed to do with that information? Should I try and find her and find out what the hell she was talking about? Should I tell someone?

The sun continued setting. It had a strange beauty. That was the weird thing about Kings Cross, it wasn't Tower Hamlets with the tiny little narrow backstreets and the pigeons gathering on the rooftops, near the chimney pots, and the swelling of St Pancras' spire in the distance, head up and proud, in the fading sunlight, there was a beauty. Depraved as fuck. I'm not denying that. But a beauty none the less. I remembered what Nadina said about looking at the sun and imagining you were in love. It was getting chilly, so I walked back down and through the courtyard and out of the exit, I was looking forward to getting back to David's and slobbing on his sofa.

Then I saw the ambulance just outside the entrance. A solitary bird sat on a chimney nearby. Black clouds drifted across the early evening sky.

The sun had set.

I didn't have to see it to know.

But I could see it.

I could see Nadina visible on the stretcher. Dead. Bright red blood all over her body which they were covering before they lifted her up. The ambulance doors shut. The ambulance drove away.

That was it.

There was no one else around to witness this, the very end moment of her life. I stood alone in the middle of the road.

It was unfathomable.

Unbearable.

Black clouds continued to float across the early evening sky.

I felt very woozy, like my balance had gone, like I might fall over.

I knew what people would say. Kings Cross lives were cheap around here. Most or many don't get to thirty.

I thought about what she'd told me about her dad. I thought what he did was like a kind of slow murder. Cells blackening, a black fog spreading. The soul so sensitive, knowing something awful had happened, a gradual electrocution. A scream lodged in every bit of the body. But also that wasn't Nadina. She furiously fought back. Against the black fog, against the bad life. She wanted out. She was getting out.

I stared and glared at the empty sky.

Beautiful, defiant Nadina.

I chanted *nam myoho renge kyo*, like I had in Yoichi's flat.

She was a friend. I swore. I vowed I would always be one for her.

Deep as a lilac,
Sharp as the snow,
Soft as a raindrop, as a river she flowed,
Kind as a mother,
Tough as the trees,
Warm as the sunrise
As a lion she breathed,
As a lion she roared, as a lion she dreamed.
She walked in the shadows, she shook in the breeze,
May her torments now be lifted,
Her sorrows be relieved
May she stroll through laughter valleys,
May she live a life of peace.

It was early morning a few days later. The sun was rising. I hadn't slept much. This rapid eruption of violence that had led to Nadina's death was having an effect. I was spaced out and reeling. I stood watching the trains go in and out of the station from a perch in York Way. Many coming in on business, many escaping, I wondered how many were coming to buy sex. I thought of all the people coming and going, being born and dying. I could see the back of Kings Cross and the big circular ceiling of St Pancras. I watched trains leaving and arriving, it was strangely mesmerising. Birds were chirping beside me, it seemed weird that they were there. There was an evergreen bush close by and they were jumping around on it or nearby, their tails twitching. Little bits of winter sunlight glinting off the edges of the leaves.

Nadina and Mike cannon fodder in that ebb and flow. No one cared about them. They were nobodies. She had been there for me, just spontaneously. I would never forget that. Where were Nadina and Mike's families? Did they even know what had happened to them? When they were born, babies, their mums' must have had so much hope for them. Someone had killed Nadina.

That's when I saw her. Nadina. She was standing under the evergreen tree; the birds were now making a lot of noise. She was staring, her unflinching gaze. But then she smiled, she was okay. I walked towards her, happy.

Then she was gone.

Was I losing my mind? Some birds flew up into the sky. At my feet I saw a gold chain on the ground.

On it was a small empty gold heart. I had blocked out a lot of the reality of her job. For most she was the lowest of the low, someone you don't open the door to, let alone let in. I saw her as the yardstick of keeping your spirit, no matter what, someone to learn from even. Was I fool? No. But she was in danger all the time. She had never mentioned that. I hadn't got that. I picked it up, and looked at the tiny heart in my hand.

A few days after this a loud bang woke me.

Loud ferocious banging, crashing, something shattering continued from outside. David's flat was on the ground floor, it was close to us. Too close. David burst through my bedroom door, trying to look calm, but his eyes were widened, alarmed. Was this more of this escalating violence spilling onto our streets?

"What the hell?"

David went to turn on the light on but it didn't work. He flipped the switch again. *Nothing.*

"Could be a black out."

The sound of bashing and shattering continued. We went very tentatively into the hallway, still in our bed gear and bare feet. David tried the hallway light but it didn't work either.

"It's a blackout."

I nodded.

We crept down the hallway into the sitting room. As it was a basement flat there were bars on the window. We peered out. The street lamps were off, so it was hard to see anything. There was the shape of a middle-aged, tall, skinny man across the road, with a stick, bashing parked cars, smashing all the windows. Glass everywhere. It was insane. He turned, sensing he was being watched and seemed to look straight in our direction. We moved away quickly.

"Guy's a lunatic," said David.

We were just on the verge of feeling safe, the bars on the windows felt good for once, when the mad guy came over, bent down, looked through, his eyes were wired and wide.

"The cathedral of St Pancras is begging us to cleanse. We must wake up! To this holy spot, this divine land, with holy rivers running beneath, like sweet flowing meadows! Ancient saints have walked these streets; wise druids have crossed these lands, but we don't see! We must wake up! A young woman has died. An Indian princess murdered in our pastures."

This arrested me. Was he referring to Nadina? The lights suddenly came back on. The power cut was over. The man seemed startled by the brightness of the street lights. He now looked hopeless, not at all scary, lost, flaccid, his stick no more than a floppy broom.

"What have you got against the bloody cars?" shouted David.

"People have to wake up!"

"To what?" I shouted. He stared intensely at me, without blinking.

"The IRA. They have guns. They might come after you next."

71

I felt the blood slowly drain from my face. David laughed cynically seeing it as part of his mad ramblings, no longer alarmed.

The lights started coming on in the opposite flats. A couple of men appeared from the building opposite. The two guys from the other building had reached the mad guy. Blue lights swirling and the bright light from front headlamps of a car marked the police's arrival. We heard doors opening as two uniformed policemen jumped out and briskly walked over to the man.

The guy from the opposite flats came over and crouched down, peering in at us.

"You guys okay?"

I nodded.

"Who is he?" I asked the guy.

"That's Sam, lived here a long time, with his girlfriend, then he cracked up. He was sectioned, just released, now sadly probably about to be sectioned again."

"He still has a flat here?"

"We've given him a room. He's vulnerable."

I nodded. Not sure how I felt about having this guy as a neighbour. I waved goodbye and still uneasy moved away from the window.

"Won't be able to sleep now, I'm wired."

David was putting on some music to soothe us, as his face turned, it softened; his eyes showed warm concern. He came over and hugged me gently.

We stopped and looked at each other. The eye contact extended.

It was different. Something was happening between us.

But I immediately blanked it, neutered it, shut it down. Wouldn't absorb it. Couldn't. He was a brother. I liked brothers and I loved having them.

David noticed I was shivering.

"Wanna play a game of Scrabble or something?"

I nodded enthusiastically. Crazy but perfect idea.

David handed me a beer and then went out and got the Scrabble board and the letters and brought it back into the sitting room and laid out the board and word pieces.

We started playing.

He was way better at Scrabble than me.

"So, no girlfriend?"

"Dumped her. She cheated on me." He said this lightly, as he stoically rolled his eyes.

"So Mid Hope House is really Heartbreak Hotel."

"Mm." He didn't look up, focussing on the Scrabble.

"Your turn."

I looked at my letters and tried to work out a word that went with the letters on the board. I put letters horizontally on the board, making the word WIFE. I glanced at him. Kind of teasing. He put letters spelling FREEDOM under the F of my wife word. I smiled.

We played for a little while longer. Quietly thrilled. Enjoying the little letters and the little words we were creating, transporting us away momentarily from all the worries and concerns. And the fact that there was back-to-back mayhem now going on around us.

But by the end of the Scrabble, we were soothed and felt ready for our separate beds.

Next morning I noticed a flyer slipped under the door. I picked it up. It mentioned in block letters the murder of the young woman i.e. Nadina in the back alley behind the Treaderton Building and that it had been the third serious incident in or around the estate, in a matter of days. The flyer advised everyone to stay inside after 6 pm as there still were no gates to lock out non-residents. The Housing

Association committee was working round the clock to sort this out with the council. There should be lockable gates up asap. There would be a residents' meeting.

David emerged and energetically started taking out eggs from the fridge.

"Do you like scrambled eggs?"

I nodded. He smiled warmly.

He glanced at the flyer over my shoulder and skim-read it as he cracked eggs.

"Scaremongering rubbish."

We were in this DIY Housing Association, basically made up of squats in the estate that had collectivised themselves and collected very low rents. Totally independent. I didn't think they were the paranoid types.

So, were we in danger? David who was also one of them, didn't seem to think so.

I took bread from the tin and sliced it for toast.

"I watched my dad go through a long horrible death a year ago."

I turned round again, surprised at this sudden revelation.

His eyes were totally sincere and open.

"I thought you said you were going to your parents on Christmas Day?"

"I was going to my parents' house. To see my mum."

"Were you close to him?"

"He was my dad."

The toast popped up. He grabbed them. He turned smiling, pleased.

Later on I wandered up the steps to my flat. I had to get that front door fixed. I knew I should wait for the locksmith to arrive before going in but I went in anyway.

I glanced at the kitchen; it looked fine, but then out of

the side of my eye, I noticed a roll-up in the ashtray. I never smoke roll-ups. Was that stale smoke? I turned quickly to leave when coming in the doorway, blocking my exit was the mad guy who had smashed up the cars outside, the night before.

I felt dizzy.

I tried really hard not to look frightened.

He looked at me blankly. Maybe he had been sedated, his eyes had a dead look.

I wasn't sure if he recognised me.

"There is never any justice," he said in his Manchester accent.

"Okay. This is my flat. The police took you away last night... Sam isn't it?"

"They released me today."

"Which means they should be locked up."

He laughed.

"This is my flat,"

"It's Rory's and mine for now. You have your own. You need to go back there."

He stared. I could see in his eyes, I was trespassing.

Like a homing pigeon, he had gone *home*.

He clearly sensed my anxiety. Smelt it like fresh piss.

"Can I get past?"

He continued with the empty dead stare and to stand in the doorway.

"Can I get past, please?"

He stood there.

"There is no justice."

I shook my head, to indicate I didn't know what he meant.

"My baby died – in my arms."

Sam looked heartbroken. I felt sad for him. People are fragile and can just unravel, lose the strength to start again.

Unless of course he was responsible for the baby's death which sent a new wave of panic rushing.

"There is no justice. My baby did not have to die, I phoned the ambulance."

"What did you mean about guns and the IRA?"

He stared at me. There was a flicker of something. And it wasn't madness.

I could hear footsteps on the stairs.

The locksmith appeared behind him with his toolbag.

"Here to sort the door out."

"I phoned the police about the man at the window with the child. They said they might get a helicopter."

Sam then turned and walked out of the flat.

He walked heavily down the steps, his long heavy coat swaying. Was the IRA reference just more of his crazy talk? Prompted by my accent?

The locksmith stood there quizzical and a bit freaked.

"Do you want me to put an extra lock on the door for you, love?"

I went in and looked around the flat, the sound of the locksmith drilling was loud in the background. Nothing had been stolen that I could see, but my book of Blake's poetry was lying open on my ripped-up brown corduroy sofa. There was a plate with crumbs lying nearby on the ground. He'd made toast. It was one heck of a Goldilocks moment.

Feeling an intense desire for chips, I walked down to the Cross. Across the road was the majestic red-brick St Pancras Station with all its twirling spires. Beside it, its sibling with its sandy-coloured broad front, there was Kings Cross Station with the bright Christmas lights and decorations still up outside. I turned right into Burger King and saw Nadina's pimp, the Glaswegian skinhead called Steve, coming down from the counter, walking towards me.

I went to dash outside the door. He might have killed her; she had screwed up with payment from a client. He looked capable of killing for sure. He grabbed my arm, his wide eyes boggling more than usual.

"Hen, wait, wait a sec."

I looked at him. He was the only living link I now had to her.

"She's dead," I said.

"She is, hen." He looked genuinely upset. He offered me a chip. I took it.

"Who did it?"

"She was with a John."

"Who was he? You should know, you whored her out!"

"I was her business manager."

"You were her pimp!"

"I protected her. She came to me. A fuckin' hard nut faggot who wouldn't rape her or let her be raped. I'm a fuckin' drug dealer, darlin'."

"You got paid."

"So did she. You know she cared for you a lot, darlin'…"

"She said she stabbed Kieran."

"She did, hen. I was delivering gear to the Irish junkie. Your guy, was wi' him. Nadina was wi' me. No reason. Just strolled around wi' me. Your guy opened the door."

"Do not call him my guy."

"Nadina recognised him. Lost it. He told her to shut it. Started saying awful stuff, pushed her, she snapped, smashed her coke bottle and glassed him wi' it… then on Boxers Day, she took herself out."

I blinked. "What do you mean?"

"She'd told me that yous were goin' to start a band and goin' to write songs together in Greece. She wanted to be with you, hen. She knew that was ni goin' to happen. She went wi' a John she didn't know. She only ever went with regulars. Girls said he was edgy. You! You fuckin' lead her on. Broke her fuckin' heart."

I walked out.

I walked down Argyle Street, past all the sleazebag B&Bs. I broke her heart? Steve, her 'caring' pimp, could have killed her. The religious Goldilocks could have killed her. The edgy John could have killed her. But according to her pimp Steve, *I* killed her.

All my life I had tried to be good person, live with a good code. But it seemed like no one else gave a shit and I was a stupid gullible bitch, who somehow killed Nadina. I was exhausted. Disgusted. I just wanted to go and lie down and not get up.

As I got towards the end of the street, I heard clapping and music. I didn't know what it was. It sounded like a brass band, with a strong beat. It was a cold winter's day at the end of December, not the time for street parties.

I followed the sound, the claps, cheers. I turned the corner, to see Yoichi standing in the middle of the street, doing what looked like a traditional Japanese fan dance with all the residents from the buildings on the narrow street, or up applauding from the communal balconies. It was a bonkers but brilliant sight. Everyone was out clapping along to his steps and the boisterous brass band music pouring out from a ghetto blaster. A glorious surprise. He was canopied under the evergreen tree, the branches hanging protectively over him.

His arms were outstretched; a huge gold fan was in his hand. With a dignified but beaming smile, Yoichi made powerful simple moves, waving his arms up and down, in time to the music. Watching him was driving my spirit upwards like he did the fan, sweeping it gracefully above his head and round. I felt his heart, he was rousing the courage in us all, maybe he had sensed the fear.

He took a lunge forward with his leg and waved the fan again around his head. Everyone cheered. Yoichi then lunged with his other leg, another cheer. He raised his arms triumphantly in the air, then he flipped the downward golden fan upwards in one swift movement. It was beautiful. So graceful. So strong. He then stretched both his arms and fists outwards to us, passing the energy on.

That was it. Everyone ecstatically clapped and cheered, on a high.

The Housing Association people started talking through a megaphone about the curfew. So, this was the meeting that had been mentioned on the flyer. If there was any trouble we would phone or, if necessary, alert each other by waving red garments out the windows.

I caught Yoichi's almond eye as he stood intently by them. He smiled over at me. I had turned that corner just in time, my spirit that had been flagging was revived.

David appeared from the other side of the crowd and rushed towards me with his cheerful energy. He looked excited. He loved the feeling of everyone together.

David pretended to do his own version of the fan dance raising his hand with his imaginary fan, lunging forward with his arm and leg. I joined in. As did a little kid beside me. As I made my lunge, I was startled to see Nick, former IRA man and mate of Kieran standing by the side of the pub. My antennae went up. Had he seen me? He quickly disappeared around the corner.

Maybe the mad guy Sam was talking some sense after all. I shuddered remembering the bit about the IRA and guns. Could it be true and had seeing that actually knocked

Sam back into his insanity? What was the connection to that and the Indian princess that Sam had been going on about? "Murdered in our pastures?"

I started running.

"Blathnaid!" shouted David.

"I have to go."

He looked surprised. A little squashed. Immediately I felt sorry, but I couldn't stop.

I ran round the corner, I could see Nick was now further down the street, the main one with all the B&Bs leading to the Cross. I quickly ran down a parallel street. I stopped at an adjoining alley between the two streets, saw Nick passing. Thrilled to see him and that he couldn't see me. I got to the end of the street and very carefully looked round the corner.

Nick was standing talking to one of the prostitutes, Abbie, who I had met in Argyle Square with Nadina. He seemed to be asking her something, she was shaking her head. Steve, Nadina's pimp, came over and joined the conversation, there was intense discussion. Steve was shaking his head. Nick then took out some cash and gave it Steve. They shook hands. Nick then carried on walking quickly to the tube subway and hurriedly walked down the steps.

I followed him down the steps, keeping behind, inside the commuter crowd. Kings Cross Station is always heaving with people, so it was easy to do, as long as he didn't look round. He didn't. I got through the ticket barriers and followed him down the escalator, keeping far away but keeping him in sight.

He then walked down the escalator and at the bottom, turned onto the Northern Line northbound platform, going through Camden Town. I followed quickly but by the time I reached the platform, the tube doors were closing. Nick was standing with his back to the door, then moving down into the carriage. I jumped on, just as beeping started and the crammed doors were closing. I sat opposite him. He saw me. It was in public, a safe space. There were people sat on either side of me.

"Who killed Nadina?"

"I dunno. Did you? You seem to be the common denominator."

"What were you doing near my home just now? What was that conversation and cash exchange that just happened outside the post office?"

He looked at me with raw aggression. The heat was rising. I could see people near him were freaking out a little, locked as we were in a moving tube carriage with two people with Northern Irish accents who were getting very angry.

"WHAT WERE YOU DOING?"

"None of your FUCKING BUSINESS!"

A man beside me turned round, annoyed.

"Do you mind?"

"Yes, I do."

"SHUT UP!" said Nick.

"IS THAT IT? YOU WANT ME TO SHUT UP? IS THAT WHY YOU WERE THERE? TRYING TO FIND OUT WHERE I WAS? TO SHUT ME UP!"

"This is a Northern Line train terminating at High Barnet," the tube voice said.

"DID YOU KILL HER?"

He got up and screaming, went for me. I managed to dodge the punch but he still managed to slam the side of my head against the tube window. I was terrified. He really had lost it. I was screaming, trying to push him off as he punched me. People ran from their seats, others screaming. I was kicking him and punching him back. The rush of the train was deafening, racing at full speed through the black

81

tunnel. All I could see was his hard gaze. He was in another space, past caring, roaring.

Someone was trying to pull him off from behind. The bright electric strip lighting in the carriage shone down. My heart was like a curled fist pounding inside my chest. Male voices. I kept punching and punching. His blows came in thick and fast, but so did his face. As it came right up to mine. I managed to ram my fingers up his nostrils. I pushed him back with my hand and then pushed again, with every bit of strength I had, screaming.

"The next stop is Euston, change here for the Northern Line Charing Cross Branch."

The tube stopped. Beeping doors opening. In a lightning adrenalised state I ran through the moving mass to the open doors and jumped out. I stood on the platform, head spinning. The doors closed. Nick was staring out the tube window. I glared back.

The train pulled off. I saw my fingernails were covered with his mucus membrane. Disgusted I wiped my hand repeatedly against my jeans and ran down the platform towards the *Way Out* sign. I heard a loud screech. As it screeched, the train had come to an abrupt stop. The doors opened, but then immediately closed again. The train moved off, racing into the black tunnel.

I ran up the escalator, through the exit barriers into Euston Station, then ran through crowds of people, through the exit doors and out into the cold grey outside. Exhausted, I stopped.

I took out the gold chain with the empty heart, that I found after seeing Nadina. I kept it in my pocket.

A ray of fading sunlight landed gently upon it.

It gleamed.

I could sort of feel her, but I couldn't see her.

Call it intuition, or instinct, or some kind of inexplicable connection.

I started walking back towards the Cross.

Cars were whizzing past. Across the road, outside the post office was Abbie, who Nick had been talking to. I crossed the road, weaving past the cars. One car slowed down; a guy popped his head out the window.

"You doin' business?"

"Fuck off!" I snapped.

Abbie backed away as I approached her. Another girl, who had sores on her face and track marks on her arms, stood nearby.

Tracksuit-wearing drug dealers were hovering nastily nearby.

"I'm Nadina's friend, Blathnaid. I met you with her in the park."

She was very young but her eyes were sharp and old. She nodded. She knew that.

"I just want to know what that Northern Irish guy was talking to you about."

She shook her head.

"Please. I think he might have killed Nadina."

Not having much money, I took out the gold chain with the empty heart and offered it to her. She looked at it, stunned.

"Where did you get that?"

"I found it on the ground. In York Way."

"It's fuckin' mine!"

"What?"

She snatched it out of my hand.

"I thought I'd lost it."

I felt a bit freaked. We both stared at it.

"I thought it might have been Nadina's."

She continued staring at it.

83

"The clasp is broken, it must have fallen off," I said.

"He killed her."

"What?"

"The Northern Irish guy I was talking to."

I inhaled sharply.

"Are you sure?"

"Yes. He asked me where the Paki girl was. Steve came over and told me to piss off. Steve talked to him and then the guy disappeared. When Nadina turned up, Steve told her a regular was waiting in the alley, back of Treaderton, behind the bin sheds. I heard Steve saying it to Nadina. I was in earshot, and I felt weird as that guy was totally new, not a regular. Today he was asking me to stay quiet. Nadina apparently glassed his mate. He'd come round to her flat, told her to stay away from you, was roughing her up."

So Steve was a lying treacherous shit.

"How do you know the guy who got glassed came round to Nadina's flat?"

"That Northern Irish guy told me today. I asked. Said I wouldn't cooperate if he didn't. Some junkie showed him where Nadina lived."

I looked round quickly to see if Steve was anywhere in sight. He wasn't. But my heart was seriously banging now, heavy looking guys standing near had clocked us. I wanted to speed this up. The boggin nearby red telephone box stuffed with call girl cards, opened, a guy, with his eyes rolling in his head, exited. A small Bacardi bottle wrapped in tinfoil, a hole burnt into it, left on the floor.

"Would you tell the police that? About that guy killing Nadina?"

"Yes."

I was a little surprised.

"We have to protect ourselves. If we don't, who will?"

84

I nodded. I was going to run into the phone box and phone the police.

"We're going to do the protest in the church," she said proudly.

I glanced across the road; a policeman was walking on his own near the entrance to Kings Cross Station. This was the moment.

"What's your name again?"

"Abbie."

"Shall we go and talk to him, Abbie?"

I indicated with my eyes to the policeman. She glanced across at him. She bit her lip.

"The occupation is against the police."

"Sometimes we need them to do their job."

I felt like screaming inside for her to hurry, but stayed outwardly calm.

She hesitated and then nodded.

We then quickly moved, crossing the road, darting past the traffic. I thought about the bond of the London Irish, lost in limbo between the two countries, but strongly together. I thought about what pricks the police had been to us, I thought about how deeply loyal I had always been. I thought about the splinters and cracks in that loyalty. I was also scared. I thought about Nadina. Clearly she had been roughed up and she was protecting herself. There was no IRA involved, just Kieran and then Nick doing his dirty work. I was split in half, pulled apart, falling apart, yet finally as we reached the other side of the road, never in my confusion so clear.

We walked up to the policeman who looked slightly alarmed at being approached by two young women at that notorious spot. I could imagine Nadina tickled pink by the irony. We told him everything, quickly, rapid-fire. He asked rapid-fire questions back and then some more and then contacted his colleagues to come and quickly pick us up. All I wanted him to do was hurry. Get us out of there.

It was raining heavily now. A puddle nearby was full of red, purple, amber and green broken coloured glass, from late-night broken drunken bottles. A bit of tinsel lay nearby. As his colleagues arrived in the police car, the street lamps came on. In my mind's eye the broken glass in the puddle became a red rose, made of precious jewels and gems gleaming in the darkness. I saw Nadina's face appear, for a second, beside the rose. She was smiling.

We got into the police car. Nick was arrested later that night.

It was a belated Christmas miracle.
Justice in a place where justice didn't happen.
Victory when we'd felt utterly defeated.
I really mourned her.
But I kept the promise I'd made in my heart.
I'd been a good friend to her.
And always would be.
For eternity.

Part IV

St Pancras Sunrise

It was now a few days into January, into the New Year. The sun was emerging, blazing, roaring, over the St Pancras skyline, fighting, pushing back the dark. I stood and watched it from the rooftop.

I was still thinking about Nadina. Despite getting Nick arrested, there was something uncomfortable lingering. Her life was dangerous, those women were often walking targets for the crazies, and the police were not protecting them. But the reality is, she was not killed by a punter or a pimp but by people I knew. Maybe Steve was right, maybe she would be alive, if it weren't for meeting me. I felt sick with guilt. Yet there was no more that I could do. The sun was now up, a fearsome fiery orange cupped beneath a red streaked V sign. V for victory.

I was going to stay at Ava's for a couple of days from tomorrow. I'd had enough of the area. The place was not safe and I didn't want to get stuck there either. Just because my own crisis had been kind of blanked out and erased, didn't mean it didn't happen. I still had to get better. My plan was, now that my hand was nearly better, to stay with Ava, maybe for a week, pick up some paid trad Irish music pub sessions, which I had been doing, and get a deposit for a room in a shared house. Stabilise.

Back in the flat with Primal Scream's *Moving On Up* playing in the background, I was busily stuffing clothes, sheets and towels into black bin bags. Steve had apparently also been arrested as well as Nick. Abbie's statement to the police was holding it all together. I was actually of little importance, other than back-up for saying, *yes I had seen Nick on the day Abbie mentioned when he tried to threaten*

87

her to keep quiet and bribed Steve with dosh. Loads of crack cocaine had been found in Nick's flat, so it seemed he had left IRA paramilitary violence behind him and somehow got involved in narcotics. Or maybe was still involved in a new way. Anyway, Nick was Kieran's closest friend, so a motive of revenge was obvious.

The artists who lived on the estate, were mostly not established but had a cheery, muscular resilience. There was nothing arty-farty about them or the flowerpots they put on the communal balconies. The new girl next door was not an artist, she was fleeing a violent marriage, hot iron put on her arm, she had been in a hostel, and her flat was emergency temporary accommodation. A middle-aged geezer friend of hers called Sid, was now popping round to see her, and said he used to be a bouncer for the Krays. He also told me he had mates that did 'blueies' if I ever needed a few bob.

Just as I was packing my last bits and pieces, there was a knock on the door. I thought it might be her, as she often was knocking asking for bits and pieces. Like in the way Mike used to. I opened the door, but there was no one there. I assumed she had got bored waiting.

I was just about to close the door when I heard a cough. Everything whirled when I saw Kieran, sitting on a chair on the communal balcony. I screamed involuntarily. I couldn't take in seeing him there, when I knew he was in hospital.

"Blathnaid," Kieran said. It was his voice. Him. It was real.

"I didn't want to scare you."

I looked at him with fear and contempt.

"Well, you did."

"I want to know where I can find that girl who squealed on Nick."

"I have no idea."

He stared at me.

Neither of us moved. My body was so tense it felt it could snap. Kieran lit a cigarette; he turned and casually looked out over the balcony, blowing the smoke out, gazing down at the road below.

"There's your new boyfriend, just come home on his bike."

"He's not my new boyfriend."

"Does that not tell you something?"

I almost laughed. I also remembered something Nadina said about mistaking familiarity for safety.

"You goin' to sit there all day?"

"Well, unless you come down here for a chat."

It was charming. Seductive.

Kieran continued to smoke his cigarette. Mike's black scraggy cat came clambering up the stairs, looking even more emaciated than normal, still hoping I suppose, that Mike might come back home and feed him. It was chilling when the cat went over to Kieran.

"That was Mike's cat."

"I know. I remember. Poor Mike. Lived and died a junkie. Very sad."

Kieran stroked the cat.

"Where did he get the heroin from that killed him? He was on methadone," I said.

Kieran picked up the cat, stroked it some more and put it on his knee.

"Mike said it was curious, he used to hold it up to the light bulb, freak it out. You're very curious too, aren't you? Nick was telling me."

Kieran put Mike's cat back down on the floor and casually looked up at me.

"Curiosity killed the cat."

It was chilling.

Kieran got up, stubbed out his cigarette. He gave me a

long stare and started walking down the steps, talking with his back to me.

"I said I'd give Mike heroin in exchange for keeping tabs on you. I was giving it to him, I got him to show me where your Paki prossie chum lived. She started screaming, to leave you alone, smashed a bottle of coke she was holding and glassed me with it."

He stopped and looked back up at me.

"Fuckin' crazy bitch."

I stared back. "I heard you were roughing her up."

"Fucking back off."

He said it with such aggression, it would have been impossible not to get the message.

From the communal balcony I watched Kieran walking stiffly along the narrow street below. Mike's meagre cat following behind. Kieran turned left into the back alley which served as a short cut during the day and a cut-throat at night. I wondered what might have happened, if Nadina had been successful when she glassed him. In that moment, I wished she had.

When he was out of sight, I quickly legged it round to the church to find Abbie. I guessed she would be there. And sweet Jesus she was. And what a sight. Just awesome actually. As I walked to the top of the street, I could see Abbie standing with a group of about thirty women, mostly sex workers but some people from the local women's centre also, all outside Holy Cross a Victorian, gothic church. A couple were holding young children, all of whom were wearing Venetian eye masks, like you would for a carnival. This was the 'occupation' of the church that I had heard snippets about.

A huge handwritten banner was hung on the side of the church: "End Police Harassment Now". Abbie was holding a placard saying "Fuck you White Man. Sex workers rights,

Human rights". Another woman was holding a placard saying "Mother's need money". Some were standing in front of a compassionate-faced statue of young Mary holding a suffering Jesus. The vicar, a young guy, stood beside them, a modern-day Jesus with his Mary Magdalenes. The sheer balls of it, I wish Nadina could have seen it.

A woman from the ECP was speaking from the steps to the press.

"The policing of sex workers in Kings Cross is increasingly brutal and racist. The situation is out of control. Constant arrests. It's relentless. We've had enough!"

A loud cheer went up. I turned round. David was there taking photographs. He smiled at me and took a photo of me, which was unexpected but nice. I smiled back. Abbie was speaking next.

"We have six demands: 1. An end to the illegal arrests of prostitutes. 2. An end to police threats, blackmail, harassment and racism. 3. Arrest the prostitute killers and racists. 4. Protection, welfare and housing for women who want to get off the game."

Susan, the woman from the local women's centre finished them. "5. Hands off our children. 6. Stop arresting our partners. We won't leave the church until someone from the Home Secretary's Office comes and talk with us. We need guarantees about future police conduct."

I said, "YES!" and applauded very loudly.

An older parishioner woman turned to me.

"How am I supposed to go into the church to pray with women like that in there?"

I smiled but said nothing.

Then the press started to talk to the vicar.

"Are they seeking salvation? Or sanctuary?"

"I think the girls may have a point about police brutality. There's too much focus on condemning them and

91

not enough on the evils of society... I'm sure the Lord Jesus would not want the women thrown out of the church."

"When will this be over?"

The vicar half-laughed.

"I'm not in control of the building!"

A local skinhead yob from the flats behind shouted, "Why don't you get the police to go in and drag them out. Tear gas!"

Spotting the moment, I crossed the road and went over to Abbie, on the steps.

"I need to talk to you."

"I can't talk."

Her piercing eyes, staring out intently from her mask.

"Listen to me. You need to be careful."

"Why?" she said defiantly.

"Because the guy Nadina stabbed – Kieran – is out of hospital. He came round to my flat today, asking where he could find you as the person who grassed up Nick. And, of course, to threaten me as well. I'm your back-up for evidence, but you are the main witness."

"Shit."

"Be careful. Like really *really* careful. Maybe it is a good thing you're going to be locked up in a church."

Abbie didn't react to my black humour, but quickly surveyed the area, with her hard birdlike eyes.

"What does he look like?"

"Tall, slim, light brown hair, grey green eyes. Good-looking. Liverpool Irish accent. Around forty. Dressed today in black jeans and big black jacket."

"Forty? So old?"

I nodded. "How old are you?"

"Seventeen."

"When he was talking to Steve was there anyone with him?"

"Yeah. For a bit of it. He was older. Was carrying a black cat of all things."

I could scarcely believe my ears.

"That's him! Would you tell the police this? He is threatening us, Abbie."

"Are you jokin'? They've already threatened to slap soliciting charges on me for saying I was there. Would you? Nadina told me about that Irish guy raping you. Was that him? Why don't you?"

It was a through gritted teeth heated exchange, and people were starting to look round. I felt desolate. Reporting Kieran when there was no evidence, and would be dismissed as a domestic. But Abbie was at her limit with reporting Nick and I got that. A nearby photographer spoke to the women.

"Can you stand in a line please, ladies, so I can take a snap?"

Abbie looked at me with a sneer and walked off.

The women stood in a messy line. Smiling, they held up their arms in triumph. Most of them plainly dressed in jumpers and jeans, not their work clothes. Probably so it couldn't be 'smuttifed' by the press. Or sensationalised – 'Vice girls hold vicar hostage. The ultimate tarts and vicar party'."

They were bringing dignity to it.

I watched them with admiration. I had seen flashes of police brutality and it was ugly. Like the Yorkshire Ripper, Peter Sutcliffe, had known in a totally murderous way, it was like the police also knew most people didn't care about prostitutes. They could do whatever they liked. The more it was branded, the more they could be treated as sub-human. For them that was about policing. This was an awesome turning of the tables. The 'bad' girls who were not so bad, pushing back against some truly bad men.

Flash of the camera. Another flash.

A well-known veteran Labour politician arrived with his wife. The vicar went over to greet them. They entered the church.

A car pulled up outside at the same time. A Camden Council male official got out, presumably to go inside for talks. The press moved towards them. Abbie, in her mask, stood by the door.

"Same as usual, Phil?" asked Abbie. It got a laugh from the press. The guy from Camden Town Council squirmed. A female Camden official walked in behind them. Then all the remaining protesting women went inside the church and the doors were closed.

I walked anxiously down the street. I could see Yoichi approaching on his bike. He stopped. "How are you?"

"Not great. I've hit a brick wall."

"You are the brick wall."

"What?"

"You change, then brick wall dissolve."

"You don't understand."

"I do. Not waiting for other people to change. With strong persistent determination we ourself change, create a ripple outwards, outside changes. The bad people help you change your karma. That's it." He laughed at the expression on my face.

"Be strong. I have to go."

I half-heartedly nodded; he laughed again, waved and cycled off.

He was strong, everyone in the buildings were living under the constant threat of eviction. For some that mattered more than others. For people not born in England it was a very big deal, but it was for others also. It was a home of your own, at a low rent, in Central London. What were they putting in the water round here? Kings Cross really was more often than not a full-on free-for-all mess, but the spirit of many who lived there really was also uniquely strong.

I turned the corner to see two policemen walking towards me.

"Did you just come from the church?"

I nodded.

"Are you part of that?"

"I was just talking to one of them."

"We are arresting some of the prostitutes as they leave."

"They aren't doing anything illegal. Prostitution is not illegal."

"Occupying a church may be."

There was a stand-off. It was a nasty energy and they were blocking my path. The policeman stood there enjoying his power.

"Personally, I don't see anything wrong with stressed-out business men or sad old farts needin' a bit of fun."

"So why be so heavy then?"

He looks at me not answering.

"Is that your wind down after a hard day's work?"

I knew I was being recklessly cheeky. I regretted it the minute I said it.

"Can you come with us? I'm taking you down to the station for questioning,"

My heart stopped. Then the policeman laughed, enjoying the look of fright on my face.

"Go on," he said benevolently, revelling in his mercy.

I carried on walking, then stopped and turned. Should I say something about Kieran?

The policeman stopped and turned. He stared at me. I stared back. Funny moment.

"Nothing," I said.

I carried on walking and turned the corner into Argyle Street.

I walked from there to Rita's at the bottom of York Way She was doing one of her chanting sessions for peace in Northern Ireland and South Africa. I wanted peace. I walked past the station with all the streams of people emerging. The green man came up on the lights; I crossed the road, buzzed on Rita's door.

Upstairs in her small bedroom, we sat cross-legged and chanted for peace. There were a couple of other people there and then she read a quote at the end. And then she talked about us all transforming our own internal anger state or the destructive aspect of it.

I looked at her sitting room as I was going. It was a shared rented house, some of her flatmates were there. It looked nice. She shouted down the stairs as I was going.

"Do you want me to walk back a bit of the way with you?" she offered.

"But then you would have to walk back on your own, or I'd have to walk you back." We both laughed at the silliness of this.

I left and walked, feeling refreshed and energised, back through the Cross, up Argyle Street into Whidbourne Street, it was getting dark. I walked round the S bend, passed McGlynn's bar, the last bit before reaching my building, when to my dismay, I saw Kieran standing outside the building entrance. I felt sick. There was another guy also standing in the shadows. I thought I might throw up. The guy had his hand in his pocket. I wondered if he had a knife.

Kieran took a step towards me. I took a step back towards Mc Glynn's. There were some used beer bottles lying on the outside bar tables. Thinking on my feet, I picked one up and smashed it on the ground. Kieran jumped in shock. Needing help, needing to get attention without alarming him, I started taking my coat off, in a sexy striptease, swinging it around in the air. I think he thought I had lost my mind. I started singing loudly.

"Ten green bottles sitting on the wall. Ten green bottles, sitting on the wall. And if one green bottle should accidentally fall, there'll be nine green bottles sitting on the wall."

"Are you drunk?" he asked.

"Kings Cross girls. Best in the world!" I shouted in reply.

I glanced up at the flats' windows on both sides. Waving red garments was the signal each other that trouble was about. Kieran took another step forward. I picked up another beer bottle and smashed it in his direction, then throwing my coat on the ground, climbed on top of the picnic table, took off my red jumper, swung it around, striptease style, now in just my shirt. Kieran walked closer.

"Cut the slut stuff. Are you a tout? Are you? You know what happens to touts?"

Adrenalin was making me fearless.

I picked up another near-empty beer glass and smashed it near him. He jumped back. I was running out of bottles.

"Eight green bottles, sitting on the wall, eight—"

Thankfully, Annie the Australian opened her window and started waving a red T-shirt out the window.

"I've phoned the police, Blathnaid!"

Other windows started opening. Yoichi's head stuck out the window, twirling a red scarf like a Man United football fan.

"Fuck off!" Yoichi yelled at Kieran. I was shocked at his profanity.

More heads were appearing. Sam appeared out of my flat bedroom window, hammering a saucepan with a wooden spoon, making a terrible racket. He threw the wooden spoon at the man in the shadows and hit him on the head.

"Nice shot!" I shouted up. "But what the fuck are you doing in my flat?"

He ignored me and carried on screaming and banging

the saucepan. David walked out of his basement flat and stood on the pavement and stared at Kieran. Yoichi also appeared at the entrance, of the opposite building. As did Annie. The Asian woman from the grocery store appeared at the top of the street with a policeman. She pointed towards us. Kieran and his mate, without making any fuss, then just turned and walked away down Argyle Walk, the back alley. Just like that.

I responded with a playful bow, which got a massive round of applause from the residents. I gave them a little bum wiggle in appreciation. More applause, whistles, and cheers. Then David held out his hand and graciously helped me down from my stage.

Must have been the performer in me, I was on a high.

David then invited me back to his for a cup of tea which turned into something to eat. It was a lovely idea, and delayed also the thorny thing of extracting Sam from my flat.

I think it was then I started to really see David. I wondered, as I chatted to him while he was in the kitchen cooking, if I would have done for him what he'd done for me. He was awesome. He seemed happy to just be a brother. For a moment I wondered what it would be like if there was anything more.

As he cooked, I watched the evening news. It suddenly cut to the Kings Cross sex workers' church occupation.

"David! Come and see this!"

David came out of the kitchen, carrying two plates of food. We both watched, the women emerged out of the church, still with their masks on,smiling and looking triumphant.

"The occupation by prostitutes of Holy Cross Church in Kings Cross has come to an end. Camden Council has agreed to set up a unit to monitor the conduct of policing in the area and the number of prostitute arrests."

It then cut to Abbie talking outside the church.

She was wearing the necklace with the empty heart on it. It was bittersweet for me. I had been the messenger.

"This is a victory! It's great to be part of change," said Abbie, very proud. She was overjoyed, but also I could see a bit mind-blown and amazed, at what they had done.

David and I looked at each other and whooped and hugged in delight. I really liked that he felt like that. Not everyone would have. Or did.

"They've done it!" I roared.

"It's David and Goliath! I think this calls for a bottle of wine!" he replied as he put the bowl of pasta and pesto on the table.

"YES!"

David disappeared into the kitchen and reappeared with a bottle of red wine and two glasses. He opened the bottle with a corkscrew. I laughed when it popped. He handed me a glass and we clinked glasses.

"Cheers!"

"Cheers!"

We both took a sip.

"When I take the piss out of your accent, I'm only joking, I really like it. I don't mean it. But you don't like it. I'm goin' to stop. If I can."

I laughed at the last bit.

"Anything for you."

I smiled. That was really nice. It also made my heart flutter. There was a silence. I took a sip of wine.

"Your photos are really good."

"Thanks, they do sell, but not enough."

"You love travelling abroad, don't you?"

"Yes, I do. I like the sun. And I think England's gone down the plughole. Thatcher is a witch."

I nodded. "What else, mystery man?"

99

"Nothing really. I'm just a naturally quiet person who doesn't like himself very much."

"I like you. Very much," I replied.

"It's good someone does." He defused it.

I smiled.

"Where does your mum live?"

"Kentish Town."

"I'm really sorry about your dad."

"It was last year, fifty- six. It was cancer."

This moved me. I could feel beneath the surface a piercing unresolved pain.

"That's so young for your dad to die."

"God, we're a right misery… this is supposed to have been a celebration!"

David then suggested we go and get some chips and make chip butties. Goodness knows what made him think of it, but it was inspired. The pasta and pesto had gone cold with all the conversation. And I think he knew, from all the paper takeaway wrapping I brought back, that I loved chips.

We walked briskly down the street, talking excitedly. It was drizzling and there were few people out. The moon was high above the St Pancras spire. But with the clockface lit up, it looked like a double moon in the sky. David pointed that out and I laughed and then he pointed to some stars in the sky. I looked up, mesmerised. It was kind of relaxing to look up and get lost in the vast blackness scattered with tiny silver dots.

We got our chips, ignoring all the dark stuff outside Burger King, we didn't see it. It wasn't there that night. We then ran back with our chips, as it started to rain and we wanted to keep the chips warm. We ran through a puddle and got our legs soaked but we were laughing. We ran full speed, round the corner, to David's flat.

We stood in his narrow kitchen; he buttered four pieces of white bread and put them on a plate. I had the job of putting the chips in between and making the butty sandwich and cutting them in two. We both looked at our artwork delighted.

In his sitting room David put on some music. Slow jazz-funk. The wine had kicked in a bit.

We danced. Slowly.

We moved closer together, our bodies touching each other. We swayed slowly, sinking, sinking into the moment. His jumper was so soft and warm. The music kept playing.

Jazz, taking the bum notes, turning them, twirling them upwards into energy and life.

"Why do you not like yourself?" I asked him.

"I don't know."

"You're hardly Ted Bundy."

"Well, at least he excelled in what he was doing."

That was funny. To us anyway.

"You're very good at being a rock," I replied. "Like you've been for me. Like it sounds for your family. That's kind of heroic."

David looked up, his soul peeping from his eyes, normally not on display, hidden behind a carefully presented inscrutable front. He humbly shook his head.

"Ted Bundy's more exciting."

"Well, if you want some strangling tips... I can always introduce you to Kieran."

I was joking. Obviously. He roared with laughter. His lovely warm brown eyes creasing up, his whole face animated and happy.

We looked at each other. Could we let it in?

We ended up in David's double bed, with the colourful yellow and red Mexican rug over us, snug, womblike.

White walls and bookshelf with books and photographic equipment and a small telescope. We kissed.

A soft, sensuous deep kiss laced with desire.

We lay on David's bed, our arms wrapped round each other, fully clothed. I was so shy.

We fell asleep with the sound of the rain falling outside. It was comforting.

I didn't hear the male footsteps walk hurriedly through the rain-strewn streets, splashing through a puddle. Or the faint sound of a cat.

I didn't see the lit rag in a bottle, Molotov cocktail style, pushed through David's letter box, landing on the cloth doormat without making a sound.

I was asleep. Under water, under blue turquoise water, then sunlight hitting the surface of the sea. Swimming to the surface.

But I did start to hear the sound of crackling. The sound of crackling was now drowning out the sound of the rain. I opened my eyes. I could hear a strange whooshing sound. The sound of fire crackling, amplified. I saw smoke coming through the door. In shock, I turned to David.

"GET UP!"

I climbed over him, picked up the phone beside his bed. He looked at me as if I was mad.

I dialled 999.

"What the fuck are you doing?"

"Fire brigade..." I said.

"18 Midhope Street. NOW... NOOOOOW!" I shouted and put down the phone.

"DAVID!" I roared.

We went out of his bedroom door to see the whole flat aflame. The Molotov cocktail that had been thrown through the basement window made the whole room go up like a torch. Spreading like lightning through the highly inflammable straw matting where it had landed on the floor. Flames were spreading across the passage to the door. Mounting panic. I looked at the bars on the basement windows. Blocking our escape. The only way out.

This was death. Yet we ran round and round his flat like panicked mice, desperate to find a way, screaming through the bars and the glass on the windows that we broke, until as the smoke thickened and heat blistered, we just slowed down, stood there praying, crying, in an unspeakable terror, as the fire kept exploding and smoke blinding us and started to choke us.

I knew this was Kieran. By the time the fire brigade got there and bust down the door, we would be both dead.

I looked at the shut front door, fire raging in front of it. I turned to David. Thick black smoke was starting to block my view of him.

Yoichi's words pounded through my brain. I looked at the door and saw a brick wall. And with every single ounce and inch of determination I could muster.

"COME ON!" I roared. David looked at me.

I grabbed his hand. We charged, screaming through the fire, through the smoke, through the closed door, out into the cold air outside. I did not feel the flames. I did not feel the fire. It was one fluid motion, running through the door, through death to life, into the raw cold air outside.

It was a *very* heightened moment.

The fire brigade never came, or if it did, it was hours later. We were kept in hospital for several days. David's hands were burnt very badly. He'd turned the red-hot metal door lock with his bare hands. We had burns on our arms and legs, there would be scars but they would fade. We were alive.

Strange thing, Sam apparently arrived at the hospital

103

when I was asleep, with Aunty Pat's little Buddha statue which he had found in the debris near David's flat. He gave the nurses a fright, but they then decided he was alright. I found it when I woke up, beside my bed. What's that expression about iron forged in the flames becoming a fine sword? It did look more beautiful and stronger for it. More graceful. Albeit altered. I kept it there on the hospital table beside me. Still have it now.

Aunty Pat and I were similar in some ways, I decided.

We were both survivors.

Part V

Afterwards

I went to the police and made a report about Kieran, regarding Nadina's case, i.e. it was not just Nick. I referred to one of their own reports made after Kieran and Nick had broken into my flat and how they were taken away by the police. Abbie stood beside me. At first the police didn't take it seriously, and were very sneery, but when one of their 'monitors' came into observe they sat up and had to take notice.

The court case did happen. Abbie did nail Nick and I did my bit with her, now side by side. It also included my statement about the tube where Nick attacked me. Other witnesses in the community also came forward to say they'd seen them both. Nick, sensing he was going down for murdering Nadina, produced evidence from his answering machine that showed Kieran told him to do it. It was enough to take Kieran down with him, for several long years. So, in the end they couldn't kill Nadina, couldn't kill her spirit.

It was a rare, beautiful and sublime moment of justice, which took many by surprise. I felt a pure ecstatic undistilled delight!

As I watched Kieran's arrest, I was quietly satisfied. Of course they couldn't connect him to the arson, but this meant I was safe, for now.

Nadina still flickers stubbornly in my thoughts. We had so little time. Sometimes the most important friendships don't last a life time but can have a crucial impact at crucial times. Maybe it's not how long you live that matters, but how much value you create with the time you have. But

105

then again the raw truth still is, she should be alive. And that fact cracks my heart.

David and I did manage to get to Ava's wedding. She looked great in her white, lacy, antique bridal dress. What a sight we must have looked. I sang a wee song which Ava approved. As I did, I could see a big fat smile break on David's half-scalded beautiful face. Everything wasn't the happy-ever-after. We couldn't stay at his mum's forever. Once more we'd be thrust out into the big bad world, once more faced with the challenge of being a self-reliant adult.

I would now, for sure, look deeper. People may be worse, or better, or weaker than they present themselves. I knew now people concealed themselves, but revealed themselves in their actions and to weigh up the balance of good and bad. And to also accept some people were actually evil, simply do not have a moral compass, the users, abusers, who are consumed and devoured by their self-centred selves.

I'd also felt the other edge of the spectrum, a state of peace and calm, compassionate happiness. Like a spiritual DNA deep in us all, always there, beneath it all, a nutritious soil capable of nourishing and enriching all life. Accepting the existence of both didn't cancel the existence of the other. At all. In fact, they were in an eternal battle. In us all. Fundamental darkness and fundamental enlightenment. Just cause all people may have a Buddha nature does not mean all people live like Buddhas, for sure.

I had no job. Yet. Just part-time music work. But I had David, and he was superb. And shagging him was also gorgeous and we did, that night, after Ava's wedding. Our bodies moving in a smooth, sensuous back and forth flow, a rhythm that was like coming from the depths within us, beneath words, beneath consciousness, ebbing, flowing, a fountain of love.

The Future

My future starts now. Within.
I am the sun,
As I rise, soar,
Into the blue sky inside,
Illuminating the outside
When I can.
Not why did I lose? But how can I win?
Not where have I come from? But where am I going?
My honey is my honey. My honey is my love.
My honey is as soft as the white clouds above.
As sweet, as sarky, as funny as is honey,
As strong, as deep, as mysterious as he is,

Not where have you come from? But where are you going?
Not who did you lose? But how can you win?

Acknowledgments

I've always wanted to write a book, right from when I was
  small.

I even made a few attempts when I was a bit bigger.

But I got involved in film and happily so, and suppressed
  the desire.

When I met Debz Hobbs Wyatt at my screenwriting class
  at City, the desire re-awoke.

She told me that she was a publisher for a small
  independent press,

Bridge House Publishing with Gill James.

And they did a seasonal Christmas anthology of short stories.

Well, I plucked up my nerve and with her support as an
  editor, submitted my first

short story, *Christmas at the Cross*, for the annual festive
  collection

and it was selected and that became Part 1 of the novella
  of the same name.

And Martin Doyle, book editor of *The Irish Times*,

printed Part 1 on Christmas Eve 2019 in *The Irish Times*,
  as part of their 12 stories at Christmas.

I was so encouraged by that and then lockdown happened,

and really I no longer had any excuse.

I had time. I had a wonderful husband, Richard Yetzes,
  encouraging me and I had a story.

Part 2, 3, and 4 followed. Debz worked on them again as
  editor,

a relationship that worked very well.

Part 2, *The Little Statue.* was also published in 2020 in the
  Bridge House Christmas collection

and again in *The Irish Times* on Boxing Day.

And then Gill and Debz at Bridge House decided that they
  would like to publish the book.

*　　*　　*

Special thanks to Debz, Gill and Martin of Bridge House
     Publishing for all their help and support,
and to Martin Doyle, Books Editor at *The Irish Times*.
Special thanks must also be given to Liam Hickey for
     giving me his flat to live in and
Daisaku Ikeda, SGI Buddhist humanist who I met in
     Taplow Court at that time.
His writing which told me that greater than understanding
     the secrets of the universe,
was finding the strength to open the door of your own life.
Catia Isaia and Richard Yetzes for being such great
     readers
and special thanks to Colm O Snoddaigh for his constant
     encouragement over time.
Toby Newland for the photograph, Maria Christina
     Savioli, Geoff Robinson, still there and caretaker of
     the flame, my mum, Pauline Murphy, and my uncle,
     Oliver Snoddy, and Robert Samuels.
Chris, Sabitha, Joanna, Miles, Sasha and many more.
Of course Kings Cross today is a transformed place.
And we were so young.
I hope all who have an edgy period in their youth,
     especially young women,
get the opportunity to transform it and get older.

About the Author

Maeve Murphy was born in Belfast and went to Cambridge University.

She is an award winning and acclaimed screenwriter and film director. She has made 3 independent feature films; *Silent Grace, Beyond The Fire* and *Taking Stock*, and four short films: *Sushi* (Venice Film Festival), *Salvage, Amazing Grace* and *Siobhan*.

Silent Grace was set in Armagh Women's Prison at the time of the Dirty Protest and First Hunger Strike, and was selected to represent the UK for Cannes.

In May 2020 *The Irish Times* listed *Silent Grace* as number 38 in the "50 Best Irish Films Ever Made".

A couple of her stories were published in Bridge House Christmas anthologies in 2019 and 2020 and also printed in The Irish Times. *Christmas at the Cross* is her first novel.

Maeve lives in Wimbledon, London with her husband Richard.

Silent Grace
IFI International (2001)

Order from IFI:
www.ifiinternational.ie/film/silent-grace/

Beyond the Fire
Verve Pictures (2009)

Order from Apple iTunes:
https://itunes.apple.com/gb/movie/beyond-the-fire/id437545152

Taking Stock
Swipe Films (2015)

Order from Amazon:
www.amazon.co.uk/Taking-Stock-Kelly-Brook/dp/B01GOYS4IK

Like to Read More Work Like This?

Then sign up to our mailing list and download our free collection of short stories, *Magnetism*. Sign up now to receive this free e-book and also to find out about all of our new publications and offers.

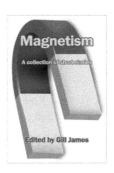

Sign up here:
  http://eepurl.com/gbpdVz

Please Leave a Review

Reviews are so important to writers. Please take the time to review this book. A couple of lines is fine.

Reviews help the book to become more visible to buyers. Retailers will promote books with multiple reviews.

This in turn helps us to sell more books... And then we can afford to publish more books like this one.

Leaving a review is very easy.
Go to https://smarturl.it/nb4on5, scroll down the left-hand side of the Amazon page and click on the "Write a customer review" button.

Other Publications by Bridge House

Wishful Thinking

by Derek Corbett

A collection of stories in which justice is not always done but leaves room for some wishful thinking.

Relationships break down ad are sometime saved by money. Snowdrops bring precious memories. Brothers in a religious order have to find a way through some difficult decisions.

Wishful Thinking is a single-author collection from Bridge House Publishing. Derek Corbett takes the reader gently by the hand and offers us the comfort of good story well told.

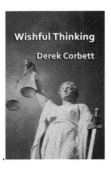

"An amazing collection of short stories, with a novella called *Glady's Time* thrown in too." (*Amazon*)

Order from Amazon:

ISBN: 978-1-907335-98-3 (paperback)
978-1-907335-99-0 (ebook)

Resilience

by Jim Bates

Remembrance Day is special for one grandfather. Which story of he and his brother at the lake will John remember today? Blake loves his garden but he's not so sure about the rabbit. Tyler stands up to his dad while hunting crows. What really did happen in the room at the Inn on the Lake? Why doesn't Quinn run away anymore?

"*Resilience* is an absolute gem. A collection of twenty-seven beautifully written short stories that deal with the central theme of its title." (Amazon)

Order from Amazon:

ISBN: 978-1-914199-00-4 (paperback)
978-1-914199-01-1 (ebook)

Whisky for Breakfast

by Christopher P. Mooney

The thirty-five stories in Mooney's debut are dominated by a cast of characters who colour outside of society's lines. They are hustlers, prostitutes, addicts, gangsters, killers, thieves, beasts. They are the dangerous, the lost, the lonely, the sick, the suicidal, the broken-hearted. Men and women, defeated by life. Their depravity is real, yet the writing in this uncompromising collection of transgressive fiction, always carefully crafted, evokes the sense that their humanity is not yet lost. In *Whisky for Breakfast*, nothing is off limits.

"A terrific read, often shocking and full of memorable characters. This is an excellent collection of short stories and would highly recommend." (*Amazon*)

Order from Amazon:

Paperback: ISBN 978-1-907335-89-1
eBook: ISBN 978-1-907335-90-7

Lightning Source UK Ltd.
Milton Keynes UK
UKHW021014111021
392014UK00009B/134